How to Fail as a Leader

A fast-paced fable about leaders who totally biff strategy and execution, but learn enough to win in the end

By Scott Wozniak

How To Fail as a Leader: A fast-paced fable about leaders who totally biff strategy and execution, but learn enough to win in the end

Copyright © 2016 by Scott Wozniak
All rights reserved.

Printed in the United States of America, First Edition.
Library of Congress Control Number 2016902879
ISBN 978-0-9837562-3-1

Publisher: Swoz Enterprises
www.ScottWozniak.com/books

ACKNOWLEDGMENTS

Like many books, this one started sloppy and scattered. Several people shared their insights with me, staying with me through rewrite after rewrite until it became a book worth reading. Thank you Mark Miller, Randy Gravitt, Andy Lorenzen, Carolyn Frakes, Rachel Wozniak, Abe Stopani, Bonnie Wozniak, Josh Hultquist, and James Cathy. Your generosity and graciousness helped tremendously and are only a couple of the reasons why I'm so glad you're in my life.

TIPS ON HOW TO APPROACH THIS BOOK

This story is based on my life—sort of. Sadly, I'm not a noble in a mountain-valley kingdom and I haven't served in the military, let alone led cavalry charges. But despite the tragic lack of sword fights in my life, the difficulties in this fable were inspired by lessons I've learned the hard way. Each chapter of the story, while full of adventure and surprises for the characters, is shaped around one of the mistakes I've made as leader.

I became passionate about leadership as a young man and learned a lot of great leadership theories. But I discovered that real world leadership demanded all sorts things the books didn't mention. In fact, in my first major leadership role, I pretty much failed. It's a good thing I wasn't a military leader because while it hurt, we all walked away alive. (To those of you who had to follow me during that hard learning season, thanks for your patience and forgiveness.) But as I processed the pain, I discovered that there were deep truths to be found in examining failure. And that when failure was used as an intense learning program, it morphed from failure into something of great value: wisdom.

There is only one thing more painful than learning from experience, and that is not learning from experience.
~Laurence J. Peter

Wise men throughout the centuries have taught that wisdom means not only learning from your own mistakes, but those of others. I've been sharing these lessons in workshops and with coaching clients for years, hoping to help others avoid the same pitfalls. Many have urged me to put these down in a form that can expand beyond what I can do in person. So I invite you to enjoy the story and in the process maybe you can harvest some wisdom from my mistakes.

Learn all you can from the mistakes of others. You won't have time to make them all yourself. ~Alfred Sheinwold

Like me, the leaders in this book learned the hard way that their understanding of leadership was incomplete. However, to make it more fun and memorable, I created a fictional medieval kingdom so our heroes could discover these insights with the fate of their nation hanging in the balance. As a result of this creative setting, any resemblance to anyone in the real world (other than me, of course) is coincidental.

Note for the experts: I replaced many of the technical terms that medieval cavalry officers would have used ("the horse is 15 hands high") with everyday language ("the horse is 5 feet high"). I wanted everyone to be able to engage the leadership issues in the story whether or not they know much about horses or military history. Thank you for your patience with the rest of us.

However, don't let the fictional nature of the story fool you into skimming over the scenes lightly, even the battles. This is not a casual story thinly covering a "teacher" writing on a white board. I carefully crafted the thoughts, actions, and even emotions of the characters. You can learn as much from the plot as from the dialogue.

Finally, to enhance the experience, you'll find at end of each chapter some ideas and questions to stimulate your thinking. You don't have to answer every question before you read the next chapter. You can just enjoy the story and come back to the ideas and questions later. However, to get the most out of the book, consider inviting a small group, or even one other person, to discuss the questions with you. Those discussions could lift your leadership to a whole new level (not to mention be a lot of fun).

Scott
WOZNIAK

THE NATION OF BOLIN

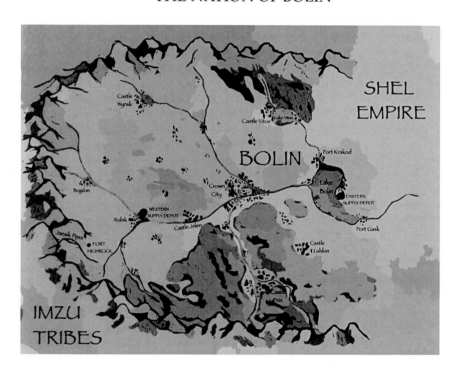

CHAPTER ONE

Addoc rode over the hill and stopped breathing for a moment. It was worse than he'd feared. He rode at the head of a company of elite cavalry, the Hussars. Being second in command placed Addoc at the front of the formation so he was among the first to see the field below them. His father rode next to him as acting company Captain, though no one called him Captain. His official titles were many, including Duke of Vitus County, First Sword of the East, and Grand Stallion in the Order of Bolin. But this group of men called referred to him as their Marshal, commanding all the Hussar cavalry companies in the nation of Bolin. The Duke surveyed the field along with Addoc. Wrecked bodies and broken weapons littered the valley. Third Company hadn't returned from patrol last night, so Addoc knew something had gone wrong. But he'd hoped it wasn't serious. After all, his younger brother, Aram, was a member of Third Company.

A flock of black scavenger birds burst into flight, obscuring Addoc's view for a moment, as one hundred horses thundered into the little valley. Addoc led a column on and his father rode at the head of his own column. Centuries of tightly controlled breeding and training, for the humans and horses, resulted in the proud and powerful Hussar forces. Steed after steed had nearly the exact same coloring—light gray coats and thick, black manes. And all of them were huge, with each horse's shoulder reaching at least six feet high and more than a few reaching seven feet tall. The cavalrymen controlling these three thousand pound forces-of-nature were noticeably tall and lean, and all wore light gray uniforms that were a near perfect match with the coat of the horses.

Birds weren't the only creature they disturbed with their entrance. A man looked up from where he was crouched on the far side of the valley. Not only did his smaller, brown horse indicate he didn't ride for Bolin, but his blue uniform identified him as a soldier from Shel. It also matched several uniforms on bodies scattered around the field. Shel, the empire that neighbored Bolin, had a well-earned a reputation for being an expansionist bully.

"You!" Addoc shouted at the man, spurring Breakaway into a full gallop, "Hold there!"

The man turned his head and froze in the middle of tugging on something. Then he scrambled onto his horse, leaving behind the body of a Bolinian soldier. Addoc didn't look too closely at what he'd been doing. He didn't want to know.

"Halt!" Addoc shouted again. "You're outnumbered! Surrender and we will let you live!" Addoc needed more information. There weren't enough bodies on the field to account for the missing Hussar company. Even as he raced toward the stranger, he was still scanning the blank faces he passed, looking for his brother. So far, he hadn't found him. Addoc dared to hope he wouldn't.

The wiry man looked over his shoulder, eyes wide, and his horse lurched away. Addoc leaned low in his saddle and Breakaway put on the extra speed for which he'd been named. In a few seconds it was clear that Addoc, who was now well ahead of the other Hussars, would easily overtake the enemy soldier. But as Addoc gained ground, the man turned in his saddle and snapped his hand backward. A knife flashed through the air just above Addoc's shoulder. This time Addoc saw the man reach for his belt, pulling out another knife. Addoc unsheathed his sword and in one smooth motion knocked the second blade aside as it flew toward his chest. The enemy grimaced and pulled his own sword out. He thrust out with his blade as Addoc rode up next to him, but Addoc easily blocked with his own sword.

As the Shel soldier made another swipe, Addoc parried the blow and followed with a counter strike that swept the man off his horse.

His rider removed, the brown horse slowed his pace and Addoc tugged on his own reins, slowing and turning Breakaway. By the time he made it back to the fallen soldier, his father and some other Bolinians had circled around the spot. The soldier was dead, whether from the fall or the sword strike, Addoc didn't know. But it didn't matter. It was too late to ask him any questions now.

Duke Vitus looked up from the body and met his son's eyes. "A bit hasty, Lieutenant, but your swordplay was acceptable."

Addoc clenched his jaw in frustration, but nodded.

"Sir," Addoc said, "Requesting permission to lead the company southeast to rescue survivors from Third Company."

"Why southeast?" the Duke pressed.

"First, that's the direction this man was riding," Addoc replied.

"He could just have been going any direction that was away from you," his father countered.

"Second," Addoc continued, pointing to specific points on the battlefield, "Third Company's tracks—that we followed—came from the west into this valley. We would have seen something on the way here if they had been taken that way. Since the only other line of tracks leads southeast," Addoc turned and pointed behind himself, "the survivors must have been taken southeast."

"Assuming any *are* alive," someone muttered.

Addoc snapped his head around, but whoever said it wouldn't make eye contact. "There aren't enough bodies on the field," he declared. "I see only about sixty to sixty-five of our men down. Unless Shel decided to bring some of the bodies with them, they took captives."

Duke Vitus nodded. "Agreed."

"Thank you, sir!" Addoc turned Breakaway around.

"Hold, Lieutenant," the Duke barked. "I agreed with your assessment of the battle, not with your plan. These men deserve a proper burial ceremony. Our perimeter needs to be fortified and messengers need to be sent back to camp. We will follow protocol and do this right."

"We don't have time for standard protocol!" Addoc blurted. "They could be just over that hill! At least let me scout the area to see if they're close."

"Read the rest of the field, Addoc. How strong was the Shel force in this battle? What equipment does it look like they used? Was this an accident?"

Addoc, now that he studied further, could see deep pits and sharpened wooden stakes. This was no accidental skirmish between patrols. Shel had been waiting for them. This valley had been prepared to defend against cavalry charge.

Seeing his son look at all the right places on the field, the Duke nodded grimly. "If you run after them, you'll likely encounter a larger force in an entrenched position. Rushing won't do any good, Addoc. After this field is secure, I'll arrange for scout teams to check the surrounding area. We follow military procedures for a reason."

"But, sir, Aram…"

The Duke looked his youngest son in the eyes. "There are only two ways we'll see your brother again: we win this war and demand the release of all prisoners, or we join him as slaves once Bolin is swallowed up by the Empire of Shel."

The Duke turned his horse around and started barking orders. Men spread out to check the perimeter of the valley while others dismounted and began pulling the bodies of their friends into an organized row, doing the gruesome work of cataloging which of their colleagues was dead.

An hour later, Addoc walked up next to his father and waited for him to finish giving out directions to another man. There really wasn't anything for Addoc to do until all the post-battle protocols had been completed. "Sir, did you have a chance to read the request I submitted a couple of days ago?"

The Duke looked at his son for a long moment. "I did."

"I think I'm ready, sir."

The Duke frowned. "Your first command is difficult in any situation. And with war imminent—"

"I've been studying leadership at the Academy for years. And with all due respect, there's not much more I can learn from being second in command, sir. And you'll need as many leaders as you can get if this becomes a full war."

But the Duke wasn't listening anymore. He was staring at nothing, thinking furiously. Why now? After years of posturing why would Shel attack now?

Ten days later, Addoc rode over the top of the hill and got his first glimpse of Fort Highrock, perched across the small valley on top of another steep hill, snug against the steep slopes of Mount Jaesik. Fort Highrock had stood guard at the far western end of the noble little country of Bolin. Stubborn and sturdy, the fort perched next to the only road leading out of western Bolin, up into the mountains behind it. The mountains drew a huge arc of impassable stone around the kingdom of Bolin, leaving only the eastern border of the country open. There was one, slim crack in that massive wall—the Jaesik Pass. Fort Highrock had kept watch over that opening for centuries. Living in the desert on the other side of the mountains were the Imzu, fierce desert nomads. Every few generations a raiding party of Imzu warriors made their way through the pass and wreaked havoc, but it had been more than twenty years since the last Imzu had been seen.

Addoc had traveled as far west as he could and still be in Bolin. The closest village, Robik, was a six-hour ride east from the fort, at the junction of two fast-moving rivers that came down out of the mountains, combined, and flowed back east. Seeing his new home, Addoc's heart sank all over again. Technically, his father had approved his request for a command of his own. But it felt more like a massive demotion. Fort Highrock was where they sent troublemakers and those wanting to retire in peace. Over the last two weeks, Addoc had gone back and forth from discouragement to anger. Seeing how small the little fort was—*his family's summer home was bigger than this*—despair welled up in him again. But he clenched his teeth and fought down the emotion. His father may have intended to put him out to pasture, safe and quiet during the war. Addoc had other plans.

Addoc's horse shook his head and snorted. Addoc's grin briefly lit up his pale blue eyes and he patted the neck of his horse. "It is pretty small, Breakaway. But we're going to do big things here." He did nothing more than shift his weight forward and his horse began trotting towards the fort. Addoc, who had been raised in the saddle, automatically moved up and down with the gait, eyes still on the fort. Yes, it was time to see what this sleepy little fort could do with a real leader's hands on the reins.

Addoc noticed the shadow of the mountain almost covering the fort and frowned. He'd have to adjust to the shorter afternoons created by a mountain range immediately to the west. He leaned further forward and Breakaway opened into a smooth canter, the huge horse's long legs easily covering the last mile to the gates of Fort Highrock.

The fort's large wooden gates stood open, each fifteen-foot tall door crisscrossed with thick iron bands. Over twenty years had passed since the gates had been tested in combat. It had grown so peaceful that a decade had passed since anyone felt the need to go through the effort required to close the gates. So they sat open, grass growing around their base.

Despite the open door policy, a soldier in a brown uniform with gray piping on the sleeves lounged in a lookout platform mounted above the gates. He shouted down to Addoc, "Who goes there?"

Addoc met his gaze and announced, "Captain Addoc Vitus."

"But…" The soldier snapped to attention. "Sorry, sir! Welcome to Fort Highrock! We didn't expect you until tomorrow, sir!"

Addoc had spent the last week and a half escorting a wagon train of food supplies to the military supply depots at Robik. With winter coming and Shel's troops already too close to the eastern supply depots, his father had ordered any surplus supplies moved out to the massive western warehouses. The River Bolin flowed down from the mountains in the west, rushing east through the heart of the country. Ships easily carried supplies back east, but moving west, against the current, required wagons—mind-numbingly slow wagons. Plodding along with the supply train stretched Addoc's patience beyond its limit. This morning, when he woke in the village of Robik, he had decided he was done traveling at wagon speed. As the drivers were hitching up their oxen, he had announced he was riding ahead and at long last urged Breakaway into a

How To Fail as a Leader

good run. The sooner he got started turning this fort into a serious strike force, the sooner he could march with them back east to join the war. Of course, riding ahead of his wagon train meant leaving behind his gear, including his dress uniform with all the markers of his rank. His current ensemble of gray slacks and white undershirt made him look no more than a private. "At ease, soldier. There's no reason you should have recognized me. You were just doing your job."

The soldier stayed at attention, but couldn't help grinning back. "I'll not argue with an officer, sir."

"Could you go find the First Sergeant for me?"

"Yes sir. I'll be right back, sir."

"No, no! Not that crate. Put that one back in the storeroom." First Sergeant Eldin hurried across the parade yard. Two privates heaved a sigh, and picked a large, wooden crate back up. Eldin continued, "This crate has winter gear, not flags." He slapped the letters scrawled on the top of the wooden crate. "It's called reading." He followed them back into the storeroom they just left and pointed to another crate while they lowered theirs to the floor. "This one. You know, the one that has the words 'Ceremonial Flags' written on it. Take it over to Sergeant Luff and he'll tell you how to set them up."

"Yes, sir."

Waiting one moment longer, to make sure they actually picked up the correct crate this time, Eldin headed toward the stables. He needed to talk to Birn about the parade gear for the horses and then get back to Sergeant Luff to make sure the flags were set up right. He'd been through a few other transitions of Captains at Fort Highrock, so he'd seen the ceremonies before. But this would be the first time he would lead the ceremony as the First Sergeant. She might be the smallest fort in the army of Bolin, but he was proud to show off Fort Highrock to the new Captain. Eldin had one more day to get all these slackers in line. Maybe that would have been enough time, but Captain Gara took all the best soldiers with him back east. Of course, that transfer created the opening for Eldin's new promotion to First Sergeant, so it wasn't all bad. But it also left him shorthanded, and the few still around were men no one else wanted.

"Sergeant Eldin!" A soldier jogged into the parade ground, waving at Eldin. Eldin stopped and waited for the man to approach. "Message from gate, sir! Captain Vitus is here!"

"What? Are you sure?"

"Yes, sir. I spoke to him myself at the gate, sir."

Eldin's heart dropped. A day early? What would the new Captain think of this mess? He looked toward the gate, a little over a hundred yards from where he stood. He didn't see any wagons or even a group. There was only a young Hussar, who looked to be a new recruit by his lack of insignia, and a few infantrymen whitewashing the walls, like Eldin had told them to. Well, Hobbs was whitewashing. As for what the other two were doing...Eldin ground his teeth together.

The gate soldier pointed, drawing Eldin's attention back to the catastrophe of the Captain's early arrival. "Right there, sir. That's him coming here now."

To Eldin's surprise, he was pointing at the young Hussar.

His blonde hair and blue eyes were common enough in the noble families, and he was looking around with the confident gaze of a leader. But that could just be the arrogance of the nobility. If he was the Captain, where was his entourage? Where was his Captain's uniform? Eldin looked down and grimaced. Did he have time to rush back to the room and get his dress uniform on?

Addoc decided not to wait at the gate, but step in and see what was going on. He saw three men whitewashing the buildings just inside the gate. They looked to be having fun, especially the skinny one, which was a good sign that morale was good. The fort really was small, smaller than any fort he'd seen, but it was arranged like all the other forts in Bolin. That meant the command center and his living quarters would be in the middle. He wasn't going to learn anything sitting still, right? Sure enough, he found the parade ground in the center, buzzing with men opening crates and carrying armloads of gear. The soldier from the gate was talking with a man in a brown uniform with a red stripe around the bicep of his sleeves. He had found the First Sergeant already. So far so good. A little shorter than average with short-cut brown hair, he looked to be in his late thirties, maybe early forties, at least ten years older than Addoc.

The stocky sergeant strode over to Addoc. "Captain Vitus?"

Addoc nodded once.

"Welcome to Fort Highrock, sir. I'm your First Sergeant, Eldin of Robik. Sir, I apologize, but we're not ready for your welcoming ceremony. I was on schedule to have the fort ready by the end of day tomorrow, though. I'm sorry for the delay. If I had known you were coming early—"

"It's alright, First Sergeant. I didn't know I was coming early until this morning. No way you could have known. The rest of men and wagons should arrive tomorrow, as planned. How about we just do a basic all-hands inspection and I can address the men that way. There's no need to go through all the trouble of a full welcome ceremony." Addoc grinned. "I'm ready to get started."

Eldin opened his mouth, then closed it. Finally he managed, "Yes sir. I can have someone take you to your room to change into uniform before inspecting the men—"

"That won't be necessary, First Sergeant. I'll just wait here while you assemble the men."

"Uh, yes, sir." The older man gave Addoc a sideways look and then walked to a large bell, hanging from a pole next to the command center building. Eldin added his shouts to the ringing of the bell, calling all hands to the parade ground for inspection. Men streamed in from all over the fort and Eldin directed the infantry as they came.

Addoc sat back in his saddle and studied his new First Sergeant at work. The Captain of a fort led the entire fort, but he wasn't supposed to directly manage the foot soldiers—not in the way he would get involved with the operations of his fellow Hussars. That was the First Sergeant's duty. The Captain and First Sergeant were supposed to work together, as commanding officer and executive officer, the top leader and his right hand man. So the leadership style of his First Sergeant mattered to him. So far, he liked what he saw. Eldin utilized names and, while firm, he didn't seem to need personal insults or vulgar metaphors to get the men to move.

Hussars flowed into the stables, which were next to the parade grounds, and emerged mounted. Eldin didn't command them, as it wasn't his place. Everyone ended up in the right place, though Addoc grimaced when he saw how few men Captain Gara had left behind. It made sense that they'd bring as many men to the warfront as they could, but it made Addoc's job much harder.

Spearmen and Hussars finally settled into columns, making a giant "V" on the parade ground, with the Hussar cavalry on their mounts to Addoc's right and the infantry to his left.

Eldin turned to Addoc and snapped to attention. "Sir! Your men are ready for inspection, sir!"

"Thank you, First Sergeant." Addoc clicked and Breakaway strolled into the space created by the inspection lines. "I'm Captain Addoc Vitus. As you can see, I'm not one for much formalities and I don't really want to inspect your lines or your uniforms today—I'm not even in uniform right now myself!" He grinned and gestured at his dusty slacks and undershirt. No one else smiled. "It doesn't matter what you look like. What matters is winning battles. Of course, you know your previous commander, Captain Gara, was reassigned east to lead a Hussar company in the war against Shel. But that doesn't mean that those of us left here are out of the war. In fact, starting tomorrow, we're going to start working on some new tactics that might just be the key to winning this war. I think you'll like what I've come up with."

Addoc figured that was enough for a first address. Besides, he couldn't think of anything else to say. "That's all for today, men. Dismissed."

For a moment nobody moved. Then Eldin stepped forward and the formation broke up. Eldin waved and shouted. "You two, over here." He waved at the two soldiers he'd just been working with. "Go get that crate with the flags and put it back in the storeroom."

They looked at him as if he had asked them to steal a nobleman's horse.

"You heard me. Move it!"

The two soldiers exchanged one more indignant look, but both grabbed an end of the crate and started walking. Eldin made a mental note to check later to see if the right crate actually made it back to the storeroom.

Addoc signaled for Eldin come closer. "Where is the Captain's stall?" Addoc asked. "I'd like to get Breakaway out of his tack and give him a good dinner. We rode hard today."

Eldin opened his mouth. Never mind about the introduction of officers, and the ceremony of transferring command to the new Captain. Never mind that Eldin had worked his tail off for years, waiting for his turn to show off his fort to the new Captain. After a moment he finally replied, "This way, sir."

Eldin walked a dozen paces and opened a large stable door, revealing a long row of stalls, each large enough for the great steeds of the Hussar cavalry. As usual, the stables were bigger and constructed with better materials than any other building in the fort. Eldin led Addoc and Breakaway down the row of stables, stopping to gesture through an open door.

"This is Birn, our Stablemaster. He'll take care of you and your horse." A boy in his late teens lifted his head from a tangle of leather and metal in the tack room. As Birn turned and stood, Addoc failed to keep the surprise off his face.

Birn was younger than any other stable master Addoc had seen before. He was tall with broad shoulders, but still lean in the way of young men who haven't filled out with muscle yet. But it was his coloring that shocked Addoc. Unlike the tanned skin and brown hair of Bolinians, Birn's pale skin was covered in freckles and his hair was a wild mass of orange-red curls. Birn's ancestry was obvious.

"I've never spoken with an Imzu before," Addoc blurted. "How long have you been in Bolin?"

"My whole life," Birn shot back. "I was born in Bogdan village, three days north of here, and I've been serving in the army for over four years. I'm as Bolinian as you are...sir."

"Captain Vitus is the oldest son of Duke Vitus," Eldin reprimanded. "Do not forget your station, Birn."

"No," Addoc raised his hands to forestall any further comments from Eldin. He hated to trade on his father's name. "Our Stablemaster is right, First Sergeant. Here, in this fort, we're all just Bolinians doing our duty—whether that's as Captain or Stablemaster." He looked directly at Birn, "And while the Imzu people may be different from us, that doesn't make them less human than we are. I meant no disrespect, Birn. Please accept my apology."

Birn's indignation was swept away by surprise. "Uh…yes, sir."

"So, which of these is the Captain's stall?" Addoc asked.

Birn pointed, "Captain Gara used the last stall on the right, closest to the command building entrance."

"Thank you," Addoc responded.

"If you want to get your horse settled, I'll be right along with your Captain's ceremonial gear—as soon as I finish repairing it." Birn gestured at the worn equipment he'd been working on, each item with the fort's emblem prominently displayed. "Captain Gara took the main set with him."

"Actually, you don't need to bother with that," Addoc countered. "I have my own equipment. I never did like the standard military equipment." He patted his mount's neck. "When I knew I was coming out here, I had some custom gear made for Breakaway. Just bring me some feed—with oats, preferably—and I'll take care of the rest."

"Uh, yes, sir."

"Excellent. Then I'll let you get back to your work." Addoc nodded at Eldin. "First Sergeant."

Eldin saluted, "Good night, sir."

Addoc returned the salute and Birn watched him lead Breakaway to the Captain's stall. "His father is Duke Vitus, the Hussar Marshal? He sure doesn't act like he's the son of a

Duke, let alone the son of the toughest Hussar in Bolin." Birn shook his head and grinned. "This is going to be the easiest Captain we've ever had. He won't care what we do as long as his horse looks good."

"We'll do a good job no matter what." Eldin reprimanded. But it didn't come out as firmly as it should have. Eldin found it hard to criticize Birn for saying what he'd been thinking himself.

CHAPTER ONE DEBRIEF

Don't judge a book by its cover. That's good life advice and you'll be a better leader if you follow it. However, I learned the hard way not to go too far. When I was a new leader I decided that the world should ignore my "book cover" and get to know the real me. So I spent as little effort as possible on my clothes or hairstyle or anything like that. For better and for worse, my natural bias is to focus on ideas more than objects, strategies more than tools. For years I didn't pay any attention to how I presented myself. And for years that impacted my ability to influence.

There is a reason we need to remind each other not to judge a book by its cover. People—myself included—can't help making conclusions about people in the first few moments of meeting them. The old fairytale of Puss In Boots is a dramatic example of this. A poor young farmer, in the times of kings and castles, came to own a clever, talking cat. This Puss, who wore Boots of course, arranged for the good-hearted young man to meet some nobles while wearing very fine clothes. Farmers didn't wear those kinds of clothes. So they decided he must be a nobleman as well. With the cunning cat's help, the farmer leveraged these new relationships to become a nobleman, complete with his own castle. He changed his clothes, which changed the way others treated him, which changed his life.

Fun as that story is (I left out some great parts), it does raise a serious question. Is it fake to plan what first impression you want to make? Are we supposed to be con artists, like the fairytale farmer? Not at all. Planning your first impressions is only fake if the message you're sending is fake.

If I'm speaking to a group of bankers, what kind of message would I send about me if I showed up in a t-shirt? Maybe by the time I finished they would respect me for the quality of my ideas, no matter what I'm wearing. But I would have created an extra hurdle for them. And some of the most successful venture capitalists in the world literally won't meet with people who show up in a suit. They only trust company founders in t-shirts. It's not about the clothes. One shirt isn't better than the other. It's about the message you are sending with your clothes.

Addoc could care less about wearing a formal uniform. That speaks well about his self-image. But not realizing the message his appearance sent to his soldiers speaks poorly about his understanding of leadership. Great leaders care more about how to connect with those they lead than what shirt they're wearing.

DISCUSSION QUESTIONS

These questions will help you explore how the main theme of this chapter shows up in your life:

1. What impression do you think Addoc made on his new command? What do they think and feel about him at this point in the story?
2. What impression do you want to make when you meet people you're trying to lead?
3. What could you do differently (clothes, hair, words, handshakes, etc) to communicate your message more clearly?

ACTION IDEA

List 3-5 friends you trust to tell you the real truth. Imagine what impression you made the first time you interacted with them. Then ask each of them what their first impression of you actually was.

How To Fail as a Leader

BONUS QUESTIONS
There are more ideas to unpack in each chapter than what's covered by the main discussion questions. So I've included bonus questions for those interested in learning from the deeper nuances of the story.

4. Addoc was dismissive of the welcoming ceremonies. How important are ceremonies? What benefits do ceremonies offer? What problems can they cause? What's your natural bias toward ceremonies?
5. Addoc didn't want to use the standard issue gear for his horse. What message(s) did that send to Birn and Eldin?
6. Addoc also didn't want help caring for his horse. What message(s) did that send to Birn and Eldin?

My answers to many of these questions can be found on my blog. To join the discussion visit www.ScottWozniak.com

CHAPTER TWO

"Where is he, Eldin?" If Sergeant Kamid wasn't such a big man with a deep, rumbling voice Eldin, might say the man was whining. His dark hair was starting to show spots of gray and his dark eyes were challenging Eldin to answer, as if it was his fault that the Captain was late.

Eldin met the older man's gaze. "I don't know. And that's *Sergeant* Eldin."

Kamid just huffed and looked away.

In the day and a half he'd been at the fort, Captain Vitus hadn't done any real work, not that Eldin could see. The young noble had wandered around the fort, asking questions and writing in the little journal he carried around with him. Eldin had seen him standing at the guard post above the gates, staring out into the mountains for long stretches of time, apparently doing nothing. The view wasn't really that special.

At dinner the night before, the Captain finally called an officers meeting for 9:00am this morning. So every one of the officers got to the command building at ten minutes before nine. But Captain Vitus wasn't there. So the four officers of Fort Highrock sat in awkward silence. And were still sitting there thirteen minutes later, waiting for their Captain to come to his own meeting. He was probably off somewhere, talking to the visitor that came in last night.

"Well, I'm not going to wait around all morning for his Dukeyness to join us," Sergeant Kamid mumbled. Sergeant Luff nodded in agreement, but neither left.

"He's not a duke," corrected Lieutenant Paldabert. Like all the others in the room, he had only been promoted last week, when Captain Gara took every existing officer and soldier of any skill at all with him. Being First Lieutenant of the Hussars was the equivalent of First Sergeant among the infantry. But since all noble-born soldiers served as Hussars and all commoners became infantry, he was the only one in the room qualified to speak on blue-blood protocols. In Paldabert's case, he was the third son of a count. Tall and lean, with straight blond hair pulled back into a collar-length pony tail, Paldabert spoke the way he lived, quiet and precise. "Being the son of a duke doesn't make him a duke. He won't become Duke Vitus until his father dies. If he wasn't our Captain, we would call him Lord Vitus."

"Whatever," Kamid rolled his eyes.

Sergeant Luff replied, even though he hadn't said anything, "Yeah, sorry."

Eldin acknowledged Paldabert's information with a quick nod. They were far from friends, but Eldin was trying to set a good tone with him. While Paldabert's noble birth meant he far outranked Eldin in society at large, as the senior leader of all the foot soldiers, Eldin ranked as a peer to Paldabert in the military hierarchy. Traditionally, in day to day operations each would leave the other alone. The Hussars had their own side of the fort and the infantry stayed on their side. But it never hurt to keep the nobles happy.

Eldin took a big breath. "I suppose we have to start without our new Captain." He picked up the stack of papers in front of him and started handing them out to the others. "I worked on these last night. Until we're back to full strength, our patrol schedules have to adjust. It means extra work, but smaller squads traveling longer routes can still get the job done."

Kamid snorted. "It's not like there's a real threat. None of the savages have the courage to cross the pass."

"We will do our job anyway," Eldin asserted.

"It's been twenty years since one of the mongrels has dared show his face around here—well, a full-blooded one,"

Kamid amended. He dropped the sheet Eldin had just handed out. "Who says we even need to do patrols at all?"

"Good morning!" a voice said from behind them. They turned to see Captain Vitus enter the room, smiling and with a spring in his step.

"Welcome to Fort Highrock," Paldabert graciously offered.

"Sir," Eldin handed his Captain a piece of paper, "I was just showing the others how we can maintain our patrol routes, if we make some changes to—."

"Whoa, there," the Captain laid the paper down on the table after one only a glance. "Let's not get bogged down in the details just yet. We can worry about details like routes and schedules later. We have bigger topics to discuss first. I've been looking around, getting a feel for the men here."

"We've done our best," Eldin quickly explained. "Captain Gara took almost all of the experienced soldiers with him. So while it looks like we've gotten behind—"

"Oh, I'm sure you've been keeping your men busy," Addoc assured him. "And many people mistake keeping the men busy with good leadership. But I want to do more. I want to inspire each of these men with a fresh vision for what they could become, for what this fort could become. Without clear vision, we risk exhausting ourselves doing the wrong thing. I'd rather be sitting backwards on a horse traveling in the correct direction than the other way around, right?"

Eldin had no idea how to respond to the nonsense coming out of Addoc's mouth. Fortunately, Addoc wasn't actually looking for a response. Unfortunately, that was because he was still talking.

"Let's begin with our purpose," Addoc said. "Why does Fort Highrock exist?"

He stopped and looked around the room. Apparently this time he actually wanted a response.

"We run patrols?" Sergeant Luff suggested.

"Yes, but why do we run patrols?" Addoc countered.

"That's what we do," Eldin answered. "It's what we've always done."

"Okay," Addoc tried again, "but what got you here won't necessarily get you where you need to go."

Kamid slowly turned toward Eldin with an incredulous look and Luff suddenly had a "coughing" fit.

"We're looking for Imzu raiders, coming through Jaesik Pass," Eldin tried to get the conversation back on a sensible trail.

"That's closer," Addoc encouraged. "But why do we look for Imzu raiders?"

Eldin frowned. *What answer was this guy looking for?*

Paldabert spoke slowly. "Our patrols deter the Imzu, keeping them on their side of the pass. This approach has worked for nearly twenty years now."

"Right," Addoc finally said. "We exist to keep the Imzu on their side of the pass. But do you know that when I asked the regular soldiers at this fort why they went on patrol, not one of them gave that answer."

"I don't care if they know why," Kamid declared. "I just want them to obey the flaming orders for once."

"That's exactly the kind of mindless obedience we need to break free from," Addoc corrected. "We've got to train soldiers to think for themselves, to find another way to reach their goals that doesn't include riding right into a headlong fight." Addoc turned over the sheet Eldin had given him and began writing on the blank backside, "I think we just identified our purpose, 'Keep the Imzu on their side of the pass.' Let's identify our values. What do we value, gentlemen?"

The silence was longer this time.

"I don't understand what you want me to say, sir," Luff admitted.

"Our purpose," Addoc began, "is why we exist, what we're trying to accomplish. Values are the beliefs and habits we want to follow while we accomplish that purpose. If purpose is our ideal 'what', values are our ideal 'how'."

Sergeant Luff blinked.

"So what are our values?" Addoc asked again. "Let's brainstorm some ideas and after we have a list we can discuss them to select the few that best represent the culture we want to create. How do we want to operate while we get our work done?"

What followed was the most awkward ten minutes Eldin's life. Well, second most awkward. Trying to kiss the baker's daughter when he was fourteen was hard to top. They said stuff like "do it fast" and "no complaining" and "pick up the right crate." And the new Captain wrote everything down. He scribbled all over the sheet Eldin had spent a good chunk of time preparing, never once looking at the patrol schedules on the other side. At long last, the Captain circled a few things on the page and put his pen down. "This is a good start. This process takes time. Keep chipping away at it and you will craft a truly powerful vision statement." He looked around the room. "I don't know Captain Gara personally, but I've heard he was a traditional officer—very hands on."

Eldin nodded. That was Captain Gara alright. Demanding, but fair. And never asking for more from his men than he did himself.

"Well, I'm not like Captain Gara," the new Captain said. Kamid opened his mouth but Eldin kicked him under the table before he could say anything stupid. Captain Vitus didn't seem to notice. "I'm interested in the big picture, not the details," the Captain declared, "Besides, you all probably know more about how to schedule patrols than I ever will. As your leader, I want to do more than just make sure all the tasks are done."

Eldin blinked. *What else would the Captain be doing, if he wasn't helping the work get done?*

"It's the difference between leadership and management. Details, like patrol schedules, are what managers care about. I'm not going to be your manager. Leaders go beyond day-to-day operations. Leaders cast a vision for a better future. Leaders create change. I am going to be your leader. Management is about doing things well. But leadership requires thinking about doing the right things."

Addoc leaned his shoulder into Breakaway's side and pulled the saddle buckle tight. His first meeting had gone well. His officers had a lot to learn about leadership, of course, but today had been a good beginning. There were a few choppy moments, but he'd known before he arrived that changing this sleepy, little fort wouldn't come easily.

Addoc walked Breakaway to the door leading out of the stable and stopped. He'd been so impatient to get riding that he hadn't thought about where he would ride. After a full day getting to know his men and preparing for his first leadership team meeting, he needed some real exercise. There had to be good trails that Captain Gara used. He glanced down the row of stalls, but no other Hussars were in the stables. Looping the reins around a nearby post, he spoke to Breakaway, "Hold on, boy. I'll be right back. The Stablemaster should know the good riding trails."

He walked deep into the stable, poking his head in stalls and equipment rooms. Sure enough, after a minute he heard the Stablemaster's voice, "I did clean it, sir. I don't know how it got dirty again."

"And I'm supposed to believe a half-breed's word?" A second man's voice answered, thick with scorn. "With your spotted skin, you probably don't even know what clean looks like."

"I do know what—"

Addoc walked a little faster.

"Don't contradict an officer! You want to be a soldier? Start with following orders."

"Yes, sir."

"That's what I'm talking about. And now, I'm ordering you to lick these boots clean or…"

Addoc stepped into the doorway and found Sergeant Kamid holding a pair of marching boots in front of Birn's face.

"Or you'll do what, Sergeant?" Addoc's voice snapped like a whip. Kamid turned his head and froze. Birn's face flushed red with shame. Kamid's face flushed red, but Addoc thought it was for another reason.

"Go on," Addoc demanded. "Explain which approved discipline procedure you'll use to force a Stablemaster to perform a duty that we require every soldier in the fort to do themselves, even Hussars. I'd also like to hear what you're doing over here in the stables at all, Sergeant. This should be interesting."

Kamid looked down at Birn and his face twitched with raw emotion. His frustration burned hot, but he had been caught out of bounds by his commander and he knew it. He lowered the boots, turning to face Addoc. Kamid's voice trembled, but he spoke slowly and carefully. "Yesterday, the Stablemaster volunteered to clean my boots, sir. So I came over here to discuss how—"

"Yes, I heard some of that discussion, sergeant," Addoc interrupted. He looked at Birn, eyes downcast, fists clenched at his side. "Stablemaster, while I appreciate your...*offer* to assist Sergeant Kamid, as your Captain, I'm ordering you to withdraw your help." He turned his head back to Kamid. "I think this is an opportunity for you to lead your men by example, Sergeant Kamid. At Fort Highrock, even our leaders clean their own boots. Don't you agree?"

Kamid spoke in a low rumble, "Yes, sir."

"Excellent." Addoc stepped out of the doorway and gestured down the hall. "Then get to it, soldier. You've got boots to clean and men to inspire."

Kamid shot one more look at Birn, as if it had all been his fault, then hurried out of the room.

Addoc watched him leave and then turned back to the young man. "Are you okay, Birn?"

"Yes, sir."

"I don't allow mistreatment like that in my command, from him or anyone else. If someone troubles you like this again, you let me know."

Birn just nodded.

Addoc was still thinking about Sergeant Kamid as he led Breakaway out into the parade grounds. As he was about to mount, he saw Eldin emerge from a nearby door in the command building.

"First Sergeant!"

"Yes, sir?"

Addoc waved him over. "I just came across Sergeant Kamid attempting to force our Stablemaster to clean his boots, rather than do it himself. Do you know anything about this?"

Eldin clenched his fist. "No, sir." But he could believe it. Kamid had been a hothead before he was made Sergeant. Now...

Addoc interrupted Eldin's thoughts. "What's Birn's story? He says he's from Bogdan, but he looks like an Imzu."

"His mother was captured in the last of the Imzu raids. She was rescued, but not before, well, when they found her she was pregnant. No one wanted to marry her after that. She had a hard life."

"Had?"

"Yeah, she died when Birn was a boy, maybe ten or eleven. Fever, I think. He ended up living in the stables of their village inn, started learning horses there. He showed up to enlist at our fort when he was still fourteen. Obviously, that didn't happen, but he has a real way with the animals, so they put him in the stables. When Captain Gara went east, he took the old Stablemaster with him, so I made Birn his replacement."

"Most people wouldn't have made someone that young Stablemaster, let alone one with Imzu blood," Addoc stated.

"He gets the job done, sir," Eldin defended. "He's been here longer and worked harder than any of the other stable hands. He earned it fair and square. What he looks like isn't important to me."

"Well done, First Sergeant." Addoc mounted and turned his horse towards the open gates.

"Sir?" Eldin called out.

Addoc looked back over his shoulder, impatient to get free of his first day and think. "Yes?"

"I was actually coming to find you—about the patrol schedules."

Addoc glanced at the open gates and sighed. "Now really isn't a good time, Sergeant."

"I need to post the weekly patrol schedules, sir. May I bring them by your office later? Captain Gara always reviews them before they were posted."

"Sure, I'll look at them later."

"When would you like for me to come by, exactly?"

Addoc sighed again. "Dinner is at sunset, right? I'll be back by then. I'll look over them while we eat."

Addoc didn't wait for another question to delay him and swung onto his saddle. Breakaway took his cue and launched into full gallop, flying out of the fort as fast as they could go. When Addoc reached the gates, he realized he still hadn't asked anyone about trails to ride. Oh well. Details, schmetails. He'd find his own trail.

The sound of pounding on wood jerked Addoc awake. He looked around in sleepy confusion. Just when he laid his head back down, someone knocked on his door again. He staggered to the door and opened it. Eldin stood there, uniform perfectly crisp, holding a stack of papers. Addoc blinked at him. "What is it?"

"I came by last night, sir, after dinner, to show you the patrol schedules, but you weren't here. The men will expect them right after the sunrise inspection."

"Oh. Patrol schedules. Um, come on in." He walked back into the room and waved at him to enter. "Sorry about that. I rode through Jaesik Pass yesterday afternoon—wanted to see what exactly we're guarding against. I started back a little before sunset." He shrugged and chuckled. "Turns out the sun sets hours later on the west side of the mountain pass than it does here. So by the time I managed to get back dinner was long over and I just went to bed. I forgot all about the patrol schedules."

Eldin followed him into the room. Addoc looked around his room and grinned. "I'd offer you a seat, but..."

His quarters had the standard military bed against one side wall, an equally standard desk against the other, and an armoire directly facing the door. Three wooden crates sat on the floor next to the armoire. Papers covered the desk, including a large stack of unanswered letters, with a sheathed sword laying over the piles of papers. Clothes filled the chair next to the desk, while boots, a belt, and books lay on the floor near the bed. Back home, Addoc's servants would have cleaned everything for him. The mess didn't really bother him, but he was beginning to realize how much work they'd done for him over the years.

Eldin held out the stack of papers. "The first two pages follow our usual routes, just with smaller patrol squads," Eldin spoke formally. "But the last two pages have some new routes I—"

Addoc ignored the offered papers and fished some socks out of the pile of clothes. "Let's use the standard routes for now."

"You don't need to look at them?" Eldin protested.

"No. I bet you did a fine job with the standard schedule. What time is it, sergeant?"

"Almost sunrise, sir," Eldin supplied.

Addoc grimaced. "Now which crate has my dress uniform?" He finally looked up at Eldin. "Was there anything else?"

Eldin stood to attention and saluted. "No, sir."

"Dismissed."

At the precise moment the edge of the sun touched the horizon, Eldin bellowed, "Attention!" and the men snapped upright. Ramrod straight himself, he declared to Addoc, "The men are yours to inspect, sir."

Addoc began to walk down the line of soldiers, trying to look confident and strong. The stern face of his father flashed into his mind and he pushed the thought away quickly. That train of thought wasn't likely to help him feel more confident. And he needed to project all the confidence he could, since he never did find his dress uniform jacket in any of his crates. In the end, he gave up and walked out in the pants everyone wore, with only his suspenders and undershirt on the upper half of his body. He had to suppress a smirk at the irony of inspecting his troops' uniforms while he was out of uniform. But protocol required that the Captain of a fort conduct sunrise inspections every morning.

"Why do we do sunrise inspections?" Addoc surprised himself a bit by asking loudly. Unsurprisingly, no one answered him. "Why do we get up way too early and stand in lines every morning?" He suddenly stopped and turned to the soldier closest to him. "Do you like waking up before sunrise every day?"

The thin, balding man glanced around desperately for help, but no one made eye contact. "Uh, yes, sir?"

"You do?" Addoc frowned. "I'm not trying to trick you, soldier. I don't like getting up early. Are you one of those morning people that wake up before sunrise no matter what?"

"Uh, not really, sir," the soldier admitted.

"Right." Addoc nodded and walked further down the line of men. He turned to another man. "So why do we do daily inspections? Why should I care what your uniform looks like?"

Addoc just waited. The other man started to sweat.

"Uh, to make sure we're ready, sir."

"Exactly! But ready for what? Ready for what, soldier?" Addoc turned to face all his men. "How many of you have ever been to the other side of the pass we guard? Raise your hands."

After a moment, about five of the men out of more than two hundred lifted a hand. "That's what I thought,"

Addoc declared. "Well, we're going to fix that. Right here and right now."

Sergeant Luff turned his head and shot a questioning look at Eldin.

"That's right," Addoc announced loudly, sweeping his arms to encompass the parade grounds. "We're all going through the pass! Right now. Gear up for a day of marching and line up by squad number. I'd like to be ready to march in twenty minutes! We'll be conducting training exercises on the other side of the pass today. Dismissed!" No one moved for a long moment. Many more men than Sergeant Luff cast questioning looks at Eldin, unsure of what to do.

Eldin was furious. After waiting for hours last night—and instead of announcing the patrol schedules now they were going on a field trip? He realized the men were still looking at him, waiting for a response. He took a deep breath and barked, "You heard the Captain. Twenty minutes!"

The men hurried back to their barracks in an effort to make the deadline.

CHAPTER TWO DEBRIEF

People have strong feelings about time and task management. In the United States many people consider how a person handles these to be a character issue. They evaluate others' integrity and maturity by how soon they show up before an appointment, for example. Failing to get a task done when you said you would means you didn't keep your word—you lied. However, I have friends who are successful leaders in places like South Africa and India who find these standards absurd. They believe good leaders are gracious enough to allow others to show up whenever it works best for them.

So what's the right answer? How should leaders manage time and to do's? African style? American style? Another style?

For individuals, I think the right approach is different for each person. We all have our own unique wiring and there's not one right answer. However, this isn't a book about identifying your preferred style. This is a book for leaders. When you are a leader, your choices have a bigger impact on others. Good leaders do what best serves their people, not what best pleases themselves.

And, of course, I made some big mistakes in this area, too. I'm naturally more "African" in my approach to time and tasks. But I was born in America and often work with leaders who are strictly "American" in their view of time. (I used to joke that I was born on the wrong continent.) Early on, I was challenged about my casual approach toward time and tasks. My flexible schedule caused real trouble for those I led, sometimes disrupting the rest of their day. I struggled with this for a while, but eventually realized that if I wanted to be a good leader, this was one of the (many) things I needed change. I needed to serve those I led by working in a way that was best for them.

I engaged a leadership coach, read books, and bit by bit established a simple, but powerful system to make sure I showed up on time and didn't forget tasks. I learned to sort and respond to emails much faster, even if all I could say was, "I'll get back to you on this next week." I became more organized and disciplined than I thought possible—because that's what my people needed from me.

I also have friends who moved from America to India who had to make the opposite shift. They had to learn to schedule their day loosely, to stay calm when the plan changed, and then changed again. When you're a leader, it's not just about you. It's about those you lead.

Addoc didn't intend to create trouble for those he led. But his casual approach to time and tasks conflicted with how the fort operated. And without realizing it, Addoc was losing Eldin's trust, one missed commitment at a time.

DISCUSSION QUESTIONS

1. When you were growing up, how did your family handle time and tasks? Were they precise and disciplined? Or were they relaxed and spontaneous? A mix of both?

2. How did your growing up experience effect your time and task management style?

3. What time and task management expectations do the people you work with have? What expectations do you have of others?

4. What approach would best serve those you lead?

How To Fail as a Leader

ACTION IDEA

Identify someone who handles time/tasks/email in a way that works well in your culture. Sit down with them and ask them about their approach. Try to find at least one change you can make to be more effective in how you manage your time and tasks.

BONUS QUESTIONS

5. How well do you think Addoc handled his first officers meeting? What did he do well? What could he have done better?

6. How well do you think Addoc handled the confrontation with Kamid? What did he do well? What could he have done better?

My answers to many of these questions can be found on my blog. To join the discussion visit www.ScottWozniak.com

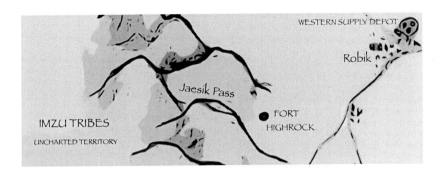

CHAPTER THREE

Addoc emerged from the winding mountain trail named Jaesik Pass at the head of a procession of soldiers, the fierce sunlight making him squint. Rolling foothills stretched out in front of him. This close to the mountain, some of the hills were pretty steep, creating a random pattern of little valleys. Instead of the low, wide trees and dark green grass of western Bolin, little more grew than tough, yellow-green grass and the occasional gnarled shrub.

Addoc led his officers to a relatively flat space just to the right of the mouth of the pass. "We'll set up a temporary base camp here," he explained. "We can leave our supplies and extra equipment here while we do the training exercises."

"Some of these idiots only brought wooden training spears," Sergeant Kamid sneered.

Addoc looked closer at the men as they marched out of the pass and assembled into two groups of infantry and Hussars. "So they did. Well, the kind of spear they have doesn't matter. We're going to work on advanced skills today, not spear thrusts."

"Speaking of, sir," Eldin asked what all the men were thinking, "what exactly are we going to do out here?"

Addoc turned to speak to his officers. "Some leaders make all the decisions and force their men to blindly obey. But in the best military squads, the men think for themselves. The leader who does all the thinking for his army becomes a bottleneck. No matter how smart or skilled he is, he can't be everywhere in the chaos of battle. So great leaders empower their people to make their own decisions."

Sergeant Kamid leaned over to Luff and muttered, "He still hasn't said what he wants us to do. Are we going to do *empowering* drills?"

Luff chortled.

Addoc nudged Breakaway a few steps forward and lifted his voice. "Men of Bolin! For twenty years, you've been looking west toward Jaesik Pass, trying to keep the Imzu from returning. But the past is over! Look around. The Imzu aren't here. They aren't coming to attack us. It's time to turn our eyes to the east—to prepare for the real threat!"

"So why did we march west?" Kamid murmured.

"We're going to run some exercises to help you make better decisions in the heat of battle. Rather than merely take orders, you're going to start thinking for yourselves. Every battle plan I've seen changes about fifteen minutes into the battle. You can't afford to wait around for your senior leaders to tell you what to do. The army of Shel is fond of setting up ambushes. So get ready to react to surprises! Oh, and speaking of surprises, I ordered the staff to break out the barrels of beer and set them up throughout the camp. Work hard today and when you're done, the drinks are on me!"

For that part, at least, the men cheered.

Addoc grinned and pointed to an oval-shaped valley spread out below their temporary camp. "Let's get started. I need half the men here and half the men there. No, not the Hussars," he waved at the horsemen who started to move forward, "you stay here for a moment. Uh, First Sergeant, can you arrange the infantrymen in two equal battle groups down in that valley?"

"Yes, sir." Eldin started calling out orders and Addoc turned to the Hussars, waving them to come closer. He dropped his voice so it wouldn't carry to the infantrymen assembling in the valley below them. "Gentlemen, just behind this valley is another one—almost exactly parallel to this one. There are two natural trails connecting the valleys. The infantry will set up in defensive formations and wait for you. I want you to head into that valley, wait about five minutes, and come back in fast. Your job is to try to surprise them by choosing a path they don't expect and get behind their defensive lines."

Lieutenant Paldabert thought for a moment, "So we could ride into the other valley at one spot and come out at another."

"Exactly." Addoc pointed to his right. "In fact, I'd suggest you leave over the southern ridge there and come back into the valley from that northern trail—which is right over there. I rode these paths just yesterday and I think you find the trails pretty easy to follow."

"Yes, sir."

"Then let's get to it," Addoc encouraged.

As the horsemen headed toward the southern end of the valley, Addoc spurred Breakaway to move into the valley. Two groups of soldiers were set up in parade formation, as if Addoc was about to do another uniform inspection.

"The men are ready for you, sir," Eldin declared.

Addoc pulled up and spoke to the whole group. "Do you see the Hussars leaving the valley there?" Men nodded. "They're going to come riding back here in a few minutes. Their job is to try to get around your defensive formations—to get the room they need for cavalry maneuvers. Your job is to try to stop them."

"Which formation would you like us in, sir?" Sergeant Luff asked.

"Good question," Addoc answered. "In fact, that's *the* question for today's exercise. You will have to decide which formation to use. In fact, I want each battle group to decide their own strategy." He pointed at the two groups, "You will be battle group one, defending the north end of the valley and you're battle group two, defending the south end of the valley. Each group should look at the terrain and decide which formation will work best to guard that end of the valley. Should you use a square, running shield, diamond? Pick the spots you think they'll attack—and be ready for surprises!"

"So it doesn't matter what formation we pick?" Kamid tested.

"Well, it does matter," Addoc countered. "If you pick the wrong formation, then they'll probably get right around you and you'll lose."

"So which one is the one that will stop them?" Sergeant Luff asked again.

"That's what you need to figure out," Addoc grinned. "I'll be watching from up here. Oh, and I'd guess you have less than ten minutes to decide." With that he rode back up to the temporary base camp to get a view of the whole area.

Kamid rolled his eyes and Eldin really wanted to join him. Instead, he turned to his men, "Alright, let's get the battle groups moving. We've got nine minutes and counting! Battle group one, you're with me."

Kamid jumped in, "Battle group two, come with me."

Eldin frowned, but didn't see a reason to countermand Kamid's choice. Kamid signaled a fast march and his men started jogging with him to the south.

Sergeant Luff looked at Eldin, "Where should I go?"

"Might as well come with me," Eldin answered.

"What formation should we choose, sir?" a soldier to Eldin's left asked.

Eldin didn't know what Addoc was trying to do with this exercise, but if it was to confuse everyone, it was working out great. "Let's start with a standard shield wall, with archers in the rear."

"Uh, what's a standard shield wall, sir?"

"No, I said a diamond formation, you morons!" Kamid roared. These lazy nags couldn't do anything right. "Brunon, you move there. Gwidon, back up, you idiot!" He'd be burned alive before he let Eldin's battle group do better than his.

"Why are we choosing a diamond formation, sir?" someone had the nerve to ask.

"Because I said so," Kamid shot back. "You got a problem with that?"

Reaching to pull another soldier into a straight line, he heard the rumble of hooves and swore. So much for having ten minutes to set up. Those cheating Hussars were early, and just as he figured, coming back on the same trail they left on.

"Set spears!" He bellowed. "Set spears! Here they come!"

The drumming of approaching horses got louder and he took one last look at his men. It kind of looked like a diamond formation, if someone had crushed a diamond into pieces. Bunch of leftover rejects couldn't do anything right.

A line of riders crested the ridge, riding a lot faster than Kamid had expected for a training exercise. And then he froze. Those weren't Hussars. He'd only heard stories, never seen them with his own eyes, but his mouth went dry and he immediately began to sweat. Time slowed and details leaped out at him.

Small steeds, some black, some brown and even tan. Robes of every color in the rainbow flapping as they rode. Wide, curved scimitars and straight, thin longswords held high. And flame-red hair.

Imzu.

He blinked and time jumped back to normal as the first line of Imzu warriors crashed into his men with reckless abandon. Almost every one of his men fell without even slowing the horsemen down. "Set spears!" Kamid screamed. About half of the second line, just in front of him, set their spears a split second before the wave of riders reached them. The other half moved too slow, failing to get the butt of their spear planted firmly in time. Some just stood there like milkmaids with their mouths open in shock. As Kamid set his own spear and angled the point forward, he snarled to himself, "Try riding through this, you red devils."

The Imzu riders crashed into a line of raised spears. Those that weren't set properly simply gave way, unable to stop the forward motion of either horse or rider. Even some of the set spears glanced off the side of horses, only scoring long, painful cuts. A few struck home and beasts fell, but too few.

Luckily, one of the handful who set their spear properly was the soldier to the front and left of Kamid. He snarled in pleasure as an Imzu rode right into the spear. And then he froze in shock as the spear broke and Imzu kept riding. It was a training spear. A burning, dog-licking, blunt-tipped training spear! Kamid was still staring at the clattering pieces of the training spear when the front of the brown horse smashed into his side, it's furiously pumping legs knocking his spear from his hands, sending him flying back.

At first, Addoc was frustrated with Paldabert. From his higher position on east wall of the valley, he could see everyone in the valley. He had told Hussars to re-enter from the north end of the valley, not the south, and they hadn't waited very long, either. But then he saw the horses. It wasn't the loose robes or the odd mix of curved and straight swords held high, or even the red hair that caught his attention first. It was the small, fleet-footed horses that his brain locked onto. Those weren't Hussars. And it was only when the first line of his men fell that he acknowledged what he was seeing.

Imzu were attacking his men. And his men were being slaughtered.

Addoc reached for his bugle and dug his heels into Breakaway at the same time. They lurched into a full gallop and Addoc began sounding a call for all his forces to regroup at his position. He watched as a few Imzu finally fell. And he squeezed his reins till his knuckles turned white as the majority of them rode out of the back of the scattered group of soldiers and wheeled around for another charge. Urging Breakaway to pour on even more speed, he sounded the call again.

There were easily forty, maybe fifty Imzu warriors, every one of them mounted. And while there were a few more infantry than horsemen in battle group two, they were scattered and terrified, facing waves of running horses. Every one of those men were going to die if they just stood there. Still riding, he placed the bugle to his lips and signaled retreat. And blew it again. And again. Whether battle group two heard his call or simply wanted to run away, they began to run toward Addoc. Rather than follow the main group, the Imzu focused on a handful of stragglers and injured men, unable to retreat. Horror and anger competed as Addoc watched them surround and cut down his men one by one.

He glanced to his right and saw Eldin's group moving south and hope flared up. If he could combine his two battle groups, he would be able to make a real stand against the Imzu. If the Imzu would just give him time to form up, he could regroup and turn this fight around.

Sergeant Kamid, running with the rest of his men, reached the place where the two battle groups were merging and looked around. His hands were shaking with adrenaline. Feeling the strength of his men around him, he started screaming at the Imzu. "Come here and try that again, you cowards! Is that all you've got?! You think you've won!? Come on!! We're ready for you, this time! Or are you too scared?!"

"Sergeant Kamid!" Addoc barked. "Shut up and get in formation!" They weren't ready yet. Men were still running into position, hardly anyone's spears were set—they needed just a few more minutes.

But Kamid's taunts struck a chord. The Imzu, every one of them, charged, wailing a strange battle cry. His men reacted with their own screams, some defiant and more than a few terrified.

Eldin's voice rang out, "Set spears! Form a line and set spears! Archers, set arrows!"

Addoc stowed his bugle and pulled out his sword. The Imzu were fifty yards away and picking up speed. The rumble of approaching hooves was louder than he'd expected. Forty yards away. He shifted his feet in the stirrups, getting a firm grip. Thirty yards away. He spurred Breakaway, building up speed to meet their charge. The pounding of hooves grew impossibly loud. Suddenly a company of Hussars flowed over the hill to his right, lances extended at full gallop. The men's cheers took on a whole new tone.

The giant, gray Hussar steeds crashed into the startled Imzu like a hammer blow. Lances shattered, blood burst into the air, and men and mounts screamed. With practiced efficiency, the Hussars dropped what remained of their lances and drew swords. Steel swung up and down and by the time Addoc had reached the group, most of the Imzu had fallen to the shock attack. Only one Hussar had fallen.

The last fifteen raiders did some quick math and fled back the way they'd come. Addoc reached the site as the Hussars regrouped, but just before they could launch into pursuit, Addoc sheathed his sword and grabbed his horn, sounding the order to fall back to camp. Addoc couldn't be sure if there were more Imzu out there and the rest of his men were clearly not up for a fight.

"Lieutenant, take your Hussars and secure the south entrance to the valley! First Sergeant, see to our wounded and dead! Once our men are all accounted for, we fall back and regroup at the fort!" His voice filled the valley. "In less than an hour, I want everyone moving back through the pass!"

Addoc rode back through Jaesik Pass at the head of a very different procession. Rage, shame, fear…they had all washed over him. But as his adrenaline finally receded, his strongest sensation was bone-deep exhaustion. He felt like crawling down a hole and waiting for it all to go away.

How could he have missed an entire tribe of Imzu? That couldn't have been a random raiding party. But he didn't really know how big a full warrior band was. Maybe it was a random encounter. Maybe he hadn't seen anything yesterday because they weren't there yesterday. He knew the Imzu were nomads, constantly moving livestock to fresh grazing. In fact, if the reports were true, there wasn't a single city in their whole country.

But why did they attack? There had to be some reason. He thought about what it might have looked like to the Imzu, and the blood drained from his face. He had marched a small force of poorly trained and improperly armed infantry onto enemy land. And when the Imzu engaged, his Hussars had swept in from the side and crushed them in what must have looked like an ambush

Had he just started a war? Bolin couldn't afford two wars at the same time.

Had he accidentally done to the Imzu what Shel had done to his brother?

CHAPTER THREE DEBRIEF

Every activity and organization has core activities that everything else depends on. Baseball is built on throwing and catching. Accounting depends on arithmetic. Painters mix primary colors to create the right shade. These fundamentals aren't especially exciting. None of the professional artists I know signed up because they love mixing paints. But these skills are called "the fundamentals" for a reason.

Many leaders are drawn to strategy and vision. I am. As a result, there was a season when I wanted to blow past the basics as quickly as possible so I could get to the more enjoyable strategy work. But a brilliant strategy executed poorly fails every time. I've lived through that painful crash more than once. This wisdom, I'm sad to say, I acquired after going through several rounds of failure. On the other hand, every field has an example of someone who achieved greatness simply by executing better than everyone else.

Vince Lombardi might have been the greatest football coach of all time. He turned the Green Bay Packers into the most dominant NFL team of the 1960s. He once said, "The *sweep's* our basic play. Everybody knows it. Everybody expects it. Everybody thinks they can defend against it. To prove them wrong, we have to execute perfectly." And they ran that same sweep, often several times in a row, all the way down the field—all the way to the Super Bowl.

It's easy to marvel at Disney World's creativity. They've earned that. But what I find even more amazing is how well they execute the basics. If you've ever been to a Disney theme park, think back. Did you see any trash on the ground? Any dirt or leaves fallen on the streets? If you're like most people, you probably didn't notice the large number of cleaning staff and the many, many trash cans strategically placed. But you can be sure that you would have noticed if

How To Fail as a Leader

trash stuck to your feet and half-eaten food spilled out of trash cans.

Addoc tried to get his soldiers to think for themselves, rather than merely follow his orders. This is a noble goal, one that the best military leaders all over the world would support. That's how the Navy SEALs operate, for example. But Addoc's men didn't even know the basic military formations. He wanted to inspire and empower them. But ignoring the fundamentals to focus on strategy only confused and frustrated them.

DISCUSSION QUESTIONS

1. What are the fundamentals in your organization—the key skills and behaviors that everything depends on?
2. What's your process to train those behaviors?
3. On a scale of 1-10 (10 being mastery), how would you rate your organization on executing the fundamentals?

ACTION IDEA

Find a way to measure how well your organization is executing the fundamentals. Even a too simple or fuzzy number is better than no measurement. And then, have regular conversations with your team about the score. This honest conversation is the main value of the measurement anyway.

BONUS QUESTIONS

4. What happens if you under-direct people who don't know what to do?
5. What happens if you over-direct people who are capable of deciding for themselves?
6. Which are you more likely to do, over-direct or under-direct?

My answers to many of these questions can be found on my blog. To join the discussion visit www.ScottWozniak.com

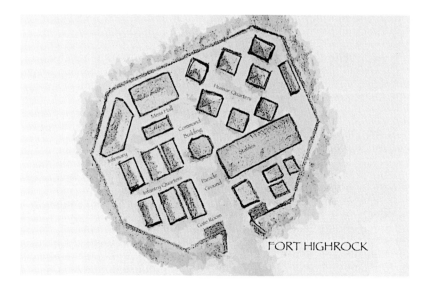

CHAPTER FOUR

The large gates of Fort Highrock issued deep groans. The men strained harder and clusters of grass that had grown around the base of the gates were ripped up by their roots. The ten foot high gates finally moved, dragging on the ground, complaining the whole way. And for the first time in over a decade, the gates of the fort were closed and locked.

Addoc turned from the gates, still riding Breakaway, and made for his quarters, but had to stop when he got to the parade grounds. Soldiers' gear littered the ground and nearly all the infantry clustered around stations with barrels and mugs. He'd completely forgotten about the celebration he'd planned. Addoc didn't have the heart to tell them to put away the beer. Truth be told, he also didn't know how the men would respond if he gave that order. Maybe it would do the men good to get a little drunk and blow off some steam.

Addoc heaved a sigh and steered Breakaway around the parade grounds. He didn't have time for a drink. Now that his men were secured, he had to figure out how to keep a war from starting.

Twenty minutes later, he placed a bucket of oats in front of Breakaway and as his horse began to crunch greedily, he collapsed onto a stool in the stall. If he could figure out a way to reach the Imzu, somehow talk to them, then maybe war could be avoided. But how did he even start that conversation? They attacked today without any warning, no chance to say a word.

Leaving Breakaway to his dinner, Addoc left to find some food for himself. He swung the stable door open and it slammed into something—someone, actually. Eldin stepped around the door, rubbing his arm and muttering something Addoc couldn't hear.

"Oh, sorry Sergeant. I didn't see you there," Addoc explained. "I was just heading to get some dinner. Why don't you join me and we can talk then?"

"I've already eaten, sir."

"Right. The galley is open then?"

"No, it's not," Eldin clarified. "I packed a travel-ready meal when we left this morning, so I ate that."

"Did all the men do that?" Addoc hadn't thought to bring so much as a snack with him and he was ravenous.

"That's part of what I wanted to talk to you about, sir. I'd like to lead a squad to the supply depot just past Robik."

"Are we out of food? When did that happen?" Addoc demanded.

"We have enough food for regular operations, sir. It's not daily operations I'd like to discuss," Eldin admitted.

"Why do we need more supplies, then?" Addoc pressed.

"We were saved out there by a lucky arrival of the Hussars, sir. But we were losing." His voice caught and he had to swallow. "Thirty seven men died today because we were caught unprepared and improperly equipped. Once we have enough food—"

"We don't have a supply problem," Addoc blurted. "You've got to stop managing details when there are bigger issues to deal with."

"Bigger issues? Details like supplies are what got us into this problem!" Eldin shot right back. "You led us into a war zone with training spears!"

"I didn't tell the men to bring training spears!" Addoc defended.

"You didn't tell them not to! And you did say it was a training exercise," Eldin spat out. "Those details you keep dismissing determined who lived or died today!"

Addoc's mouth hung open. He'd forgotten whatever he'd been about to say.

Seizing his advantage, Eldin grit his teeth and tried again. "One squad and four wagons is what I think we need, sir."

"Four wagons? How much extra food do you think we possibly need?"

"Little things," Eldin asserted, "like having enough food for the army to stay on the field for at least two weeks, will decide whether our attack on the Imzu will succeed or not."

"The last thing we will do is attack the Imzu again!" Addoc declared. "We've got to stop a war, not start one."

Eldin's mouth hung open.

"If I can just find a way to make contact with them, open diplomatic channels, I can—"

"The war already started!" Eldin corrected.

"One skirmish doesn't have to result in war. I know this isn't what you want to hear, after today, but you have to trust me on this. It's not too late."

"And why should we trust you!?" Eldin exploded. "What have you done to earn that trust? From the spearmen to the stablemaster, the men are afraid of what crazy idea you'll come up with next!"

"That's it!" Addoc clapped his hands together. "Where is our Stablemaster?"

"Birn?"

"Do we have another stablemaster I don't know about?"

"What do you want Birn for?"

"I've been trying to figure out how to approach the Imzu without sparking another attack. But, maybe if they see what looks like one of their own with me, they will be willing to talk before attacking." Addoc was getting excited. "All I need is one minute of conversation with their leader. The right idea at the right time can change everything."

Eldin couldn't believe his ears. "You want to ride back there just to talk to them?"

"It's called diplomacy, Sergeant," Addoc snapped.

"If you want to ride to your death, that's your problem," Eldin shot back. "But don't drag Birn down with you."

"Whether you believe me or not, I'm right about this," Addoc declared. "And I'll prove it. Bring the stablemaster to my stall. And get two days of food rations prepared for me and him." He could handle the details if he had to.

Eldin didn't move.

"Were my *orders* not detailed enough, Sergeant? Get moving. I need to make contact as soon as possible, before this escalates further."

Eldin opened his mouth, then closed it. Finally he managed, "Yes, sir," and stormed off.

Doubt flared up in Addoc. But he pressed it back down. He didn't have time to second guess himself. And he was afraid of what might happen if he allowed himself to open that door. There was too much at stake for him to break down now.

Eldin realized two facts as he marched away. First, the Captain had broken under the stress and was not able to lead them through this crisis. Second, he did need to find Birn as fast as possible. And he needed to hide him somewhere the Captain couldn't find him, at least until the Captain calmed down.

The sun had set and the mood in the fort was dark. All of the soldiers with combat experience had been taken east with Captain Gara, so most of the men left had never seen a real battle. It wasn't anything like the stories. No one was ready to go to sleep and no one wanted to be alone.

Kamid sat at one of the many campfires that had sprung up around the fort and stared into the fire. Someone passed him a jug of beer, recently refilled from a nearby barrel, and he tipped it back. It was going around the fire in a continual circle. How dare they attack him? Who did they think they were? He took a second swig from the jug. He had showed them, though! He took a third drink of beer and the man next to him nudged him.

"Come on, Kamid. Pass the jug already!"

"I'll drink as long as I want," Kamid barked. "And that's Sergeant Kamid, you puking moron." He took one more long drink, just to make his point, and then passed the jug.

You had to be firm with people if you wanted them to respect you.

"I can't believe the fifth squad is all dead," someone across the fire said. "The whole barking squad!"

"Yeah, except for Kamid, here," someone else said. "Only survivor of fifth squad. Glad I'm not in your squad, Sarge!"

The men laughed with drunken abandon, until Kamid punched the man next to him in the side of the head.

"Shut up, you pig-faced idiot!" The soldier collapsed to the ground. Kamid was a big man.

After a moment of silence, the men burst into louder laughter, one man spitting out the mouthful of beer he'd been trying to drink.

It wasn't his fault. The dirty Imzu snuck up on him, tried to kill him when he was on a training exercise. They were probably laughing at him right now, thinking they made him run away. If they were here, he'd bash the smile right off their faces.

"How'd they know we were going to be out there anyway?" Kamid asked no one in particular. "Did you think of that? Who told them that I'd be out there with a squad carrying training spears?"

No one laughed at that.

"You think we got a spy, Sarge?"

"What do you think?" Kamid barked. "You think they're smart enough to sneak up on us like that without someone snitching?"

"But how could an Imzu spy get in here?" The other man whined.

And then he knew. Kamid had warned Eldin about it, making the half-breed stablemaster, told Eldin the mongrel couldn't be trusted.

"We've had an Imzu spy with us for years," Kamid declared. It all made sense, now. "Sitting right under our noses."

The campfire went silent. In a drunken haze, the men looked suspiciously at one another, as if the spy sat right there. Sergeant Kamid spoke with such deadly certainty, such hate, that it suddenly seemed very real. Too real. They had been trying to forget the danger, but it had reared its head right in their midst.

"Uh, who is it, Sarge?"

"The stablemaster, you idiot! Do you know any other Imzu living in our fort? Who else would have known we were going over there? Shoot, he probably handed out training spears!"

"But, he's always been nice to me," the soldier wavered.

"That's what any good spy would do," Kamid reasoned. "Trick us into ignoring him, say he was one of us. But just look at him—he isn't one of us. He's probably laughing at us right now." Kamid spat. "And we don't have to take it anymore!"

The men murmured angrily.

Kamid grabbed the beer jug from one of the men and stood up, drinking long and deep. "I say we go have a little chat with our spymaster." Then he smashed it into the fire, creating an explosion of sudden flames. "Who's with me?"

Eldin stepped out of Birn's empty quarters and slammed the door shut. He thought for only a moment and headed toward the center of the fort. There was only one place Birn could be. But if Addoc found him in the stables first…he quickened his pace.

As he got close to the stables, he heard Birn's voice, talking to someone else.

He was too late.

He hurried around the corner, toward Birn's voice, and walked into the back of a crowd. An angry crowd.

Before Eldin could make out what was being said, Birn's voice was drowned out by the shouting of several, clearly drunk men. No one had seen him approach, but only because they were all focused on Birn, whose back was pressed up against the wall.

Sergeant Kamid's voice roared over the chaos. "Are you happy, huh? Or are you disappointed that more of us didn't die, you filthy Imzu? Well, you've had your fun and now it's our turn!"

The mob screamed at that, pressing closer, shoving against each other.

Eldin marched directly into the back of the crowd. "Step aside, soldier!" Eldin barked. If they heard him, they didn't do anything. He deliberately pushed himself between two men who blocked his view. One of them swore and started to push back, stopping when he saw who it was. Eldin didn't acknowledge him, already grabbing the arm of the man in front of him. He spoke as forcefully as he ever had, hoping military conditioning would break through the mob mentality controlling these men. "Spearman Bartek! Move aside!" When he finally broke through the last row of men between him and the door, he found two men were holding Birn's arms and Kamid was shouting, pressed so close his spittle was landing on Birn's wide-eyed face.

"How'd you do it, you half-breed?!" He slapped Birn hard and the men cheered.

Eldin stepped forward. "Sergeant Kamid!"

Kamid didn't even glance at him. Eldin grabbed Kamid's shoulder to turn him around and Kamid's shoved Eldin away. "Don't touch me!"

The mob went quiet for a second at the sight of their First Sergeant shoved by a junior officer.

"You are out of line, Sergeant Kamid!" Eldin thundered. He needed to get control of the situation quickly. "Release that man immediately."

The two men holding Birn's arms let go, but Kamid turned his back on Eldin and grabbed the front of Birn's shirt in his fists. "He has to pay!" Kamid snarled.

"Pay for what?" Eldin demanded.

"You know what for!" Kamid insisted. He shoved his face into Eldin's, stinking of alcohol. "And unless you're in it with him, you'll help us!"

Eldin backed up a step to get some breathing room. "If this man did anything wrong, we will address it through the proper channels."

"The proper channels?" Kamid's eyes were glassy and wild. "The proper channels?! You mean our idiot captain? We don't have time for him to get his act together." He spoke to the crowd. "This dog deserves to pay tonight!"

The crowd shouted their support. One on one, any of them would have been intimidated by the Sergeant, but the night hid their faces. And being one of the crowd at night made them feel reckless. Kamid's face split into an ugly grin and he turned back to frozen young man, seeming to forget Eldin was even there. "This stinking pile of horse dung doesn't belong here." Kamid punched Birn in the nose, knocking the young man's head back into the wall behind him.

Eldin stared in disbelief. He opened his mouth to reply when screams of a different kind erupted from the mob. Shoving men off their feet, Addoc rode Breakaway into the mass of men.

Kamid whirled around as Addoc approached, but before he could do anything, Addoc kicked him in the face. The wide-eyed men stepped away from the snorting warhorse. Eldin, hesitated for a second, then grabbed Birn and pushed him toward Addoc. Kamid scrambled to his feet while Eldin and Addoc swung Birn up into the saddle behind Addoc.

Breakaway lurched into a run, knocking aside any men in his path. Responding like a single animal, the mob ran after them. It wasn't much of a race though.

Eldin stayed where he was, trying to decide if he'd actually helped Birn by sending him with the captain.

As he rode away, Addoc looked over his shoulder to see the mob falling behind.

"Are you okay?"

"Yes, sir." Birn's eye was blackening already and his lip was bleeding, but there didn't seem to be any major damage. Addoc had pulled off the rescue easier than he feared. Except that the gates in front of him were closed. He glanced back at the trailing crowd. The idea of charging into his own men made him feel nauseous. He didn't think he had killed anyone back there. His speed had been pretty slow and he'd kept Breakaway from kicking. But the odds were small that he could make another charge through the mob and not do real harm. At the last moment, he steered Breakaway to the side and slid to a halt next to the gates. Leaping off his horse, he shouted, "Wait there!"

Stepping into the gate room to the right, he leaned into the large wheel that controlled the gates. Looking over his shoulder, he watched the mob grow closer. Slowly, the wheel began to move. It picked up speed and Addoc glanced back to see the mob gaining ground. He checked the width of the door opening and ran back to his horse, leaping into the saddle and almost knocking the stablemaster off.

"Hold on tight! This is going to be close!" The front line of soldiers was close enough for Addoc to see their faces, twisted with drunken rage. Addoc squeezed Breakaway into the narrow gap.

"Where are we going, sir?" Birn asked.

"I have a job for you," Addoc declared. "Are you up for helping me stop a war, soldier?"

"Yes, sir!" Birn sat up a little straighter in the saddle.

They were about ten yards out, and gaining ground when a horrible whistle went past Addoc. He knew that sound too well. But he never expected it coming from his own fort. Another arrow flew past his other shoulder. It missed by a fair margin. Several shafts flew out, none very close. Then one of the arrows—no one ever claimed the shot—plunged into Birn's lower back. He screamed in agony and leaned to the side. Addoc reached back, trying to stabilize him. But Birn's grip weakened and a few yards later the young stablemaster fell.

The mob went silent, stunned for just a moment at what happened. Everyone holding a bow threw it to the ground. Addoc turned Breakaway back around and locked his eyes on the group of men standing in the shadow of the gates. Someone screamed, "Close the gates! Lock 'em out!"

And the men hurried to put a wall between themselves and their captain.

Addoc leaped off Breakaway and ran up the trail to where Birn lay on his stomach.

The gate doors slammed closed, booming their denial into the night. Addoc looked up from where he kneeled, hands pressed into Birn's back, trying to slow the bleeding. He'd deal with their insubordination later.

"Stay with me!" Addoc commanded. Blood flowed through his fingers. "Come on, Birn. Talk to me!" The blood stopped flowing. At first, Addoc thought that was good. But Birn's breathing stopped, too.

Addoc pressed on the wound harder. "Come on! You can't die! Your country needs you, Birn!" He kept his hands on the wound for almost a minute longer. But finally he sat back.

He stared at the stablemaster who had never fit in and his heart broke. Birn hadn't done anything to deserve this. Tears rolled down his face and he removed his sticky hands from Birn's back. After staring at them with blurry vision for a while, he wiped them in the dirt.

What was he going to do now?

CHAPTER FOUR DEBRIEF

When Addoc needed Eldin to support him, he couldn't convince him to follow. What was the mistake that cost him Eldin's respect? Was it being out of uniform? Was it being late? Was it not communicating well about the training event?

It was none of these things by themselves. It was all of these things combined.

Little mistakes add up. Actually, they multiply. Each one isn't a big deal. But a pattern of mistakes destroys your credibility. Others trust you to the extent that they can predict what you're going to do. If they can count on your word, then they begin to trust you. If they know you well enough to know what you'd say or do in a situation, it gives them confidence.

On the other hand, being inconsistently good is almost the same as being consistently bad. Others have to take into account all the possible outcomes of working with you. So if you're inconsistent, every time you make a promise, others have to prepare themselves for this being one of the times that you won't follow through.

Trust is the foundation of influence. It sets the boundaries for how much influence you will have. And the more innovative and aggressive your ideas are, the more trust you need built up. If you want me to jump off a cliff with you, I will need absolute trust that you have taken care of all the details correctly when packing our parachutes.

I used to think the details didn't matter. And I learned (the hard way) that little things matter. In one of my first major leadership roles, I piled up a track record of small mistakes: little, foolish things like forgetting equipment and coming late and leaving the building door propped open after I left. None of those mistakes by themselves would have ruined others' trust in me. But all of them together did.

If you still think that little things don't matter, then consider a pebble in your shoe. If you need to cross the room you can endure the pebble. But if you want to travel a long distance even a baby pebble becomes a big problem. The repeated jabs of the pebble will add up to a ruined foot. Don't underestimate how little things grow into big patterns. Influence begins with establishing a pattern of behavior that encourages others to trust you.

DISCUSSION QUESTIONS

1. What consequences have you experienced when a leader dismissed the details?
2. What have you done as a leader that built trust between you and others in your organization?
3. What have you done that might have eroded some of that trust?
4. How much do think your people trust you? How confident are you that your guess is right?

ACTION IDEA

Maybe there are apologies you need to make to those you lead. If so, go out of your way to do it soon. And don't try to defend or justify yourself. Just apologize and ask for a chance to start over with a clean slate. Practical Tip: A good apology includes: 1) Naming the behavior you're sorry for, 2) Acknowledging how it made them feel, 3) What you'll do differently from now on, and 4) No defending, explaining, or justifying why you did what you did—that should be handled in a separate conversation.

BONUS QUESTIONS

5. What is the difference between a good apology and a poor apology?
6. Eldin didn't agree with or understand what Addoc was trying to do. Have you ever been told to lead people down a path you didn't think was the best?
7. What's the best way to handle your leader giving you direction you don't agree with? Should you pretend to those you lead that you support the idea? Or should you tell those underneath you that you would rather do it another way?

My answers to many of these questions can be found on my blog. To join the discussion visit www.ScottWozniak.com

CHAPTER FIVE

A horn rang out across the fort the next morning. The men woke to the morning reveille, groggy and hung over. For a moment, their headaches dominated their attention and it felt like any other morning after too much drinking. Then they remembered.

But before they could dwell on the empty cots next to them, the voice of their First Sergeant intruded. "Get your lazy tails up! Sunrise inspection in ten minutes!" Usually, they hated sunrise inspections, but today the demands of preparing for inspection gave them something else to think about. It made things feel normal.

Eldin knew about a dozen of the men had more than the Imzu attack on their minds. But aside from Kamid and Bartek, he wasn't sure exactly who had been in the crowd last night. And while he was seriously concerned about Kamid's behavior, he had a more urgent problem that needed to be dealt with first. Neither Captain Vitus nor the stablemaster came back, so he had to assume the worst. They were riding out to talk to the Imzu, likely to their death. And that left him to get the fort ready for a fight.

Last night, after the men had chased after the fleeing Addoc, Eldin retreated to the command building to think. What Addoc had failed to understand, Eldin had built his career on. Hard work and precision, getting the details right, were the key to success. From day one, Eldin had worked harder to master the skills of soldiering than the other recruits. He cleaned his boots until they shined—including the inside of the tongue of the shoe no one else would see. His kept his uniform perfect and could put a tent up faster than any man in the fort. In short, he became the best soldier in the camp.

Discipline and attention to detail had been the key to his success, and it would be the key to beating the Imzu. No more visionary speeches or surprise games. These men needed real leadership.

Exactly ten minutes after Eldin's wake up call, the men found themselves stumbling into lines—unshaven and wincing at the bright light, but they stood at attention while Eldin walked the line. The Hussars looked much better, standing crisply on their side of the parade ground.

"Yesterday was a day gone wrong," Eldin spoke while he walked the lines, stopping to scowl at a partially untucked shirt. The soldier hurried to fix his uniform. "Yesterday, good men died. Today, though, we're going to do things right! Look at yourselves! This is the worst morning lineup I've ever seen. And your barracks don't look any better than you. We're going to put our house in order, get our gear ready, and load proper supplies. And then, when we're acting like real soldiers again, we're going to march out and see how the Imzu handle Bolinian soldiers who are prepared for them."

Lord Paldabert cleared his throat and spoke loud enough for everyone to hear. "Sergeant, if I may ask, where's the Captain? Are these his orders?"

Eldin swallowed. With Addoc gone, the chain of command wasn't exactly clear. Did Addoc's absence make Paldabert the acting Captain? Addoc hadn't resigned. But he wasn't here, either.

"The Captain rode out of the fort last night on a mission, Lord Paldabert," he replied loud enough for everyone to hear. "He told me about his mission, which you and I can discuss later, and we spoke about the need to prepare for an invasion."

Paldabert thought for a second and Eldin held his breath. Of course, the captain hadn't agreed that they needed to invade, but he hadn't told Eldin not to prepare for it, either. He tried not to appear as worried as he really was. This was the one moment he couldn't plan for. Everything would fall apart if Paldabert decided to challenge Eldin. After an agonizingly long handful of seconds, Paldabert nodded. Eldin took a big breath and nodded back. This just might work after all. With a straight back and firm voice, he spent the next fifteen minutes walking each row of men and commenting on the smallest aspects of their appearance. He made his message as clear as possible. Every detail counted.

"Sergeants," Eldin finally bellowed. "Set your men to correcting their many mistakes and meet me in the command building in one hour. Lieutenant Paldabert, I respectfully invite you to join us as well. Dismissed!"

When the officers entered their usual meeting room in the command building, they found Eldin seated, holding a stack of paper. He nodded to each as they entered, but otherwise remained silent. When they all arrived he stood and passed out the sheets.

"This is a battle readiness plan." He handed out a page to each man. "Each of you has a list of duties to achieve before we are ready to march on the Imzu. Lieutenant," he handed a sheet to Paldabert, "in your case, of course, while I took the liberty of writing down some suggestions, you will know what preparations are best for the Hussars."

Paldabert nodded. No one spoke for a full minute as they read through their assignments.

"Any questions?" Eldin finally asked.

"Yeah, what about patrols?" Sergeant Luff asked.

"The point of patrols is to alert us to any Imzu in the area," Eldin answered. "We already know where the Imzu are. Besides, we'll need every man to get ready for our march through the pass."

"So," Luff said, "what is the battle plan once through the pass?"

"First, we establish a secure base at the mouth of the pass. We need to guard our rear. Then we send out scouts to find their camp. We don't make a move until we know where they are."

"We sure don't want to wander around the desert like idiots again," Sergeant Luff muttered.

Eldin nodded and continued, "When we do find them, we attack with everything we've got."

"Works for me," Kamid smiled. "It's payback time."

Luff chuckled.

Eldin looked at Paldabert. "What do you think, Lieutenant?" Again, his endorsement could make or break Eldin's plan.

Paldabert furrowed his brow, but said, "Sounds reasonable to me."

Eldin kept his face neutral, but confidence began to grow in his chest. "Any other questions?"

"Yeah, what's this on my list about cleanup duty in the stables?" Kamid asked.

Eldin looked him in the eye. He had worried about how to deal with Kamid, lost sleep over it when he usually fell asleep right away. He could, of course, crack down and apply the maximum punishment. One interpretation was that Kamid had disobeyed a direct order when he ignored Eldin last night. But Kamid wasn't looking at Eldin when he shoved him and maybe he was just too drunk to know what was going on. Of course, Eldin had to do something. Kamid had been way out of line. And the Imzu attack made all this harder. Could Eldin afford to lose one of the few men who had any combat experience? In the end, he decided on a middle approach.

Eldin took a breath. "Our stablemaster had to leave last night. I think you know what I'm talking about." Kamid scowled, but Eldin pressed on. "Since you've been so…concerned with how the stable is run, I thought you'd be best person to get that job done until he gets back. Do you need me to explain more?"

"Whatever," Kamid stood up. "We're done, right?"

"Yes," Eldin confirmed. "My goal is to march through the pass first thing tomorrow morning. Each of you should be able to finish your list in time, but only if you get started now." The men looked at their paper again. "Let's get to work."

Everyone else followed Kamid out of the room. Less than five minutes had passed.

Eldin walked into the bright sunlight and allowed himself a small, satisfied smile. So far, so good. That had been the best officer meeting of his career. Efficient, specific, and professional.

Addoc held the white flag high and shouted, "Parley! I want to talk!" He waited a moment and shouted again. He stood next to Breakaway, who stomped the ground impatiently. Addoc's sword lay conspicuously on the ground in front of him. He held nothing but the white flag of truce.

He filled his lungs and shouted again, calling for a parley. He shifted his feet and prepared to wait.

The sun beat down on him from directly overhead. Not knowing what else to do, he had buried Birn in a little gully just off the trail where he had fallen. He'd paced that gully for a while after that, fighting back tears of anger and shame and loss. Birn hadn't deserved to die. And Addoc wasn't going to let his death be for nothing. So he got back on his horse and rode through the night toward the pass.

It had taken him until morning to get to the other side, walking Breakaway slowly on the trail to avoid injury in the dark. But he couldn't bring himself to quit. And then another three to four hours had been spent creeping around, trying to find the Imzu tribe. He couldn't afford to blunder into a group and spark another fight. Even if he won, it would ruin his chances of a peace talk.

He didn't care if none of the other men believed him. This was the right move. And a real leader didn't choose what to do based on popular opinion.

He breathed in and screamed his call again. His arms were getting a little tired. But he didn't have to wait much longer. As he'd hoped, a small band of Imzu rode over the hill directly in front of him and halted. The four riders halted just out of the range of a bow.

"Parley!" Addoc shouted one more time, waving his white flag to drive his point home. "I seek parley! I am the Captain of the Bolinian fort! I seek to speak with your leader!"

The Imzu eyed him warily and looked around for other dangers. "You are alone?" one of them called.

"I come in peace!" Addoc returned. "I have an important message for your leader!"

They talked quietly and Addoc lowered the white flag. One of them laughed loudly and the speaker called to Addoc again. "If you come in peace, lay down on your stomach! Then we will parley with you."

Breakaway looked at him and snorted.

Addoc patted Breakaway's neck. "Yeah, buddy, tell me about it."

Addoc didn't like it, but he probably would have asked the same thing if the positions were reversed. Well, time to see if he was right about the Imzu. He put the flag down and lowered himself onto his stomach. The Imzu trotted over to him, still looking all around for a trap. Eventually, they encircled Addoc. One of them reached down and jabbed his back with the butt of a spear. Addoc grunted in response and they erupted in laughter.

"You are the leader of your people?" the speaker demanded.

Addoc lifted his head and was rewarded with another jab of the spear. Putting his head back down, he tried to speak loud enough to be heard. "I am Captain Vitus, leader of the fort just across the pass."

"Where are your men, leader?" the speaker jeered.

"They are close enough," Addoc hedged. Turning his head just enough to look at the speaker from the corner of his eye, he asked, "Are you the leader of this tribe?"

The man puffed out his chest. "I am Zishwae, the Warlord of this tribe." He was wide and well-muscled. He was the only man with a beard, and it was thick and as red as his hair. "I lead seven Chakas of warriors," he continued proudly. "How do I know you are who you say you are? Where are your warriors?"

"May I stand?" Addoc didn't wait for an answer and started to get up. As he expected, the spear thrust out again. Twisting quickly, he grabbed the shaft and yanked on it. Rather than be pulled from his saddle, the Imzu warrior let go. Swords and spears blossomed in a deadly ring around Addoc. Breakaway huffed, but Addoc put a hand on his nose, settling him back down. Moving slowly, he threw the spear down.

"I didn't come here to fight," he assured them. "I came here to stop the fighting. What happened yesterday was a misunderstanding. We did not know you were here. I only wanted to show my men what was on the other side of the pass."

"I could kill you right now," Zishwae taunted.

"And then my men would retaliate and there would be war. How many warriors will you lead after we have fought many battles? This is not necessary. On behalf of Bolin, I apologize for the loss you have suffered. I, too, lost men in the fight. If it helps, I can offer you supplies and materials in repayment for the trouble we have caused."

"We have no need of your supplies!" Zishwae's men laughed with him and brandished their still extended weapons. "We have all the swords we could want and plenty more. And how do I know you speak for Bolin? You say you are the leader, but you have no followers."

Sure enough, their equipment looked brand new. And, in addition to their traditional curved swords, they pointed spears and longer, straight swords at him.

"What can I do to prove that we aren't interested in invading you?" Addoc came close to begging. "You are safe from us. I swear to you, we will not attack. We do not want your land! You have nothing to fear from us!"

Zishwae spat. "I do not fear you! You think we fear your invasion? It is you who should fear us! It is we who will invade you!"

Addoc's heart skipped a beat. Zishwae really meant that. And none of the other Imzu looked surprised to hear his proclamation. "Then I guess there isn't anything else to talk about," Addoc offered sadly.

"Indeed not," Zishwae agreed. "Now you die."

The Imzu each pulled back their arms to strike Addoc down.

Addoc whistled and Breakaway instantly snapped his hind legs out in a kick. One hoof caught a smaller horse in the face and the other clipped the leg of its rider. The horse staggered back and the rider fell. The other warriors slashed and thrust at Addoc, but in the split second of distraction he dashed to the side of his warhorse. Using the reins to turn Breakaway—and shield himself—he whistled again and two massive legs smashed into another horse and rider. The other two Imzu hesitated. Likely, none of them had ever seen a horse this big, let alone one trained to fight as a warhorse.

Zishwae screamed, "Kill him!"

Addoc scooped up one sword and leaped onto Breakaway's back. Before he had even gotten his second foot into the stirrup, Breakaway was running.

A spear grazed his shoulder, deflecting off his armor. But with each step he pulled further away. Addoc had named his horse Breakaway for a reason. Even among the mighty Hussars, his horse was famed for his sprinting ability.

As the Imzu fell behind, Addoc laid the longsword he'd grabbed across his lap and screamed in frustration. All this for nothing. Maybe if Birn had lived, they would have listened…but he would never know. The only thing he knew for sure was that the Imzu were preparing to invade. And his men weren't ready.

As dinner approached, Eldin's plans to march the next morning seemed less and less realistic. One by one, delays popped up. The first issue surfaced only an hour after the officers meeting. Sergeant Luff came to ask about packing the backpacks. Eldin's list hadn't said how much of each item should be included. So Eldin had to create a more specific packing list for him and then send that update to Kamid's squads as well. Then Luff came back when the new list didn't all fit in the backpack. Eldin opened the offending backpack and discovered the bedroll hadn't been rolled tight enough. So he rolled it the right way and, surprise, surprise, there was plenty of room. Of course, the next guy's bedroll was done wrong, too. So he re-rolled that one. And the next one. And ended up re-rolling every bedroll in the squad. He finished that and hurried back to his own list before they could ask him to spoon feed them for lunch.

All that re-work put both Eldin and Luff behind on their tasks. Then there was the disagreement between Kamid and Paldabert on whose damaged armor the quartermaster should repair first. Eldin settled that by telling them to go in order of seniority (Paldabert, naturally), not by whose was damaged the most (Kamid's "suggestion"). Every item needed to be fixed before they marched anyway. Then, of course, Kamid refused to work on any other items on his list, glowering at the smith until he finally got to Kamid's equipment.

What Eldin really needed was a twin brother to help him out. Too bad he didn't have a twin brother. Time after time, moving from one task to another, he found men making mistakes. Stupid mistakes. These men had been left behind by Captain Gara for a reason. And time after time, he had to stop and correct their errors.

When he made it to the mess hall for dinner, the other officers were already eating. While he sat down, Luff asked the question they were all thinking, "Are we still gonna march in the morning, sir?"

Eldin frowned. "We'll march when we're all ready. Are you ready?" He looked up from his food and waited for a response.

Luff looked down at his food. "No, sir."

"But can we afford to wait another day?" Paldabert questioned.

"I'll tell you what we can't afford," Eldin declared. "We can't afford to go into battle unprepared again. We've seen what happens to fancy plans thrown together at the last minute. A disciplined army eats complicated strategies for breakfast. We'll march when we're ready to march with excellence."

No one spoke for a while after that. Eldin was fine with that. He had run out of patience for sloppy work.

Precision was the path to success and he would not step off that path.

CHAPTER FIVE DEBRIEF

Eldin was probably the best soldier in the fort. But despite what he expected, that didn't make him a great leader. That only made him a great soldier. This is true of all disciplines. I learned this the hard way the first time I directed a play. I had played major parts in dozens of plays by that time, but being a good actor didn't make me a good director. I had to learn new skills, like setting rehearsal agendas and giving enough direction to be clear but not so much I stifled the actors' creative ability. Despite my personal abilities, I couldn't get on stage and play all the parts at the same time. Leadership meant preparing them to perform well without me when the curtains went up. Eldin could pack a bedroll faster and tighter than any of his men. But what he needed was for *them* to be able to pack the bedrolls correctly.

Demonstrating how to pack a bedroll again, but with extra frustration this time, didn't really help. Maybe his men needed to be trained. Maybe they needed to be shown why it mattered. Maybe they needed better backpacks with more space. These are a few examples approaching this problem like a leader. But when Eldin packed their bedrolls himself, he had given up on leadership. Good soldiering on his part. Bad leading.

If this sounds like the most frustrating way of getting results, I know what you're feeling. I've felt this way many times. Delegation does take longer than doing it yourself. People development is never efficient. Doing it yourself will always be faster.

But I have good news. You don't have to delegate if you really don't want to. You can be a very successful professional by continuing to rely on your ability to accomplish things. But make your choice with your eyes wide open. Avoiding delegation is the choice to walk away from being a leader. Delegation and development are not optional features for leaders. The heart of leadership is making others better at what they do. While you do have to slow down at first to equip and empower your people to perform well, in the long run a lot more will get accomplished. If you want to go fast, do it yourself. But if you want to go far, do it together.

I invite you to aim for long-term success, to reach for the kind of results you will only get if you release control and empower others. I'm inviting you to shift from being an individual contributor to a leader.

DISCUSSION QUESTIONS

1. When Eldin talked with the other officers, what could he have done to delegate better in the officers meeting?
2. What could Eldin have done to empower and equip his soldiers when he saw they were struggling with their tasks?
3. Do you think Eldin or Addoc does a better job leading an officers meeting? Why? (See Chapter Two for Addoc's meeting.)

ACTION IDEA

Temporarily delegate an important decision you usually make. Let someone else make that decision a little while, maybe for a week or a month. Pay attention to how you feel before, during, and after this time. Watch what happens to the attitude and behavior of the person you delegated it to. Afterward, ask for feedback on how you could have better prepared them for success.

BONUS QUESTIONS

4. Eldin chose not to apply the maximum punishment to Kamid. Was that the right decision?
5. How do you think Eldin should have dealt with Kamid?
6. Eldin wanted more information before committing to action. What are the advantages of waiting to gather more information? What are the disadvantages?
7. What is your natural tendency, to wait too long or jump too soon?

My answers to many of these questions can be found on my blog. To join the discussion visit www.ScottWozniak.com

CHAPTER SIX

It took another full day to finish all of the preparations on Eldin's lists. But an hour after the sun rose, two days after the Imzu attack, the soldiers of Fort Highrock were finally ready to march.

Eldin waited until the gates opened all the way, settling back into the grooves created by a decade of rest in the open position. He made eye contact with Paldabert, who nodded in return.

Eldin's horn rang out and the march began. The Hussars led the way, putting their most powerful force out front where they could maneuver—and because they were nobles. Even when they were as fragile as newborn kittens, nobles walked in the front of the line. Each company of infantry marched in tight formation, their company flags snapping in the breeze. It took an hour for everyone, supply wagons and all, to get through the gates and down the hill, but at long last they were on their way with everything they needed for a serious offensive campaign. The gates finally closed behind them and the full might of Fort Highrock entered Jaesik Pass with revenge on their mind.

Eldin led the front row of infantry, the traditional position for the First Sergeant. Of course, that also meant he ate the most dust kicked up from the hooves of the Hussars, which was also the traditional role of a First Sergeant. Real leadership meant getting down in the dirt with your men. As his men moved into the pass, he began mulling over the work ahead of them. First priority would be setting up a base camp. They'd need defensive trenches and pikes around the camp. Which company should do that? The Fourth? No the Sixth would be better for that.

Eldin had been plodding through the pass for about twenty minutes, almost halfway through, when shouting erupted behind him. A bend in the pass cut off his view about fifty yards back and his line of soldiers extended much further back than that. Most of the trail allowed only three warhorses or six men to walk side by side comfortably. He pointed at a nearby soldier. "Bartek, check that out and report back here as fast as you can."

Bartek dashed back down the path, toward the fort they'd just left. The noise grew and Eldin signaled for the rest of the men to halt. When a bugle call sang out Eldin gave up waiting for Bartek. He tried to jog, but the orderly march was devolving into chaos. The closer he got, the more the noises sounded like battle. But that couldn't be right.

Ten long minutes later, pressing through the men as fast as he could, Eldin rounded the last bend, where he had just come from. In the clearing outside the pass he saw three unmanned supply wagons, their horses dancing wildly in their harnesses. Two groups of his spearmen, about ten each, clumped between the wagons and a dozen other Bolinians lay dead on the ground nearby. Just then, thirty black horses rose over a hill to Eldin's right and swept into one of the clusters of spearmen. Two Imzu were brought down, but six of his men fell to the scimitars of the white robed riders. The Imzu continued their ride through the clearing, disappearing over a hill on the other side of the valley.

These Imzu were on the wrong side of the pass.

His full predicament began to sink in. Not only were his men bottled up in the pass, the sun was in his men's eyes. They needed some time to set up a defensive wall. The Hussars!

He turned and ran back the way he'd come, shouting as he ran, "Move to the side! Against the walls! Get against the walls!"

At the end of the line, he found what he feared. The infantry were so preoccupied with finding out what was happening in the clearing that they were paying little attention to the sixty-eight Hussars stuck behind them. His own men were blocking their best chance to counter the Imzu attack.

"Lieutenant Paldabert!" Eldin called without slowing down. "Lieutenant Paldabert! The Imzu are on our side of the pass and they're attacking the supply train. We've need the Hussars back there—now!"

Paldabert grimaced. "I'm trying to move, Sergeant, but your spearmen are in my way."

"You're right. Men! Get against the side of the pass! Against the side of the pass!" They started to obey and Eldin looked back at Paldabert. "How's that?"

"You clear the path and I can have my men back to the mouth of the pass in ten minutes," Paldabert promised.

"Make it five minutes," Eldin replied. "It looked like there were about thirty Imzu. Once we're on open ground, our larger numbers should be enough to handle this raiding party."

Paldabert turned and shouted at the horsemen he commanded, "Columns of two! Riders on the right, get against the wall and let the center and left columns turn around!"

Eldin left Paldabert to organize the Hussars and addressed his own responsibility. "Against the wall! Backs against the wall! Give the Hussars room! Against the wall!"

After the nine longest minutes of Eldin's life, Paldabert and his fellow Hussars cantered around the bend, squinting into the morning sun. Paldabert blew a deep horn blast and the first wave of Hussars broke into full gallop.

The Imzu had wreaked havoc in the twenty minutes they'd been the only horsemen on the field. Eldin estimated twenty five of his men down. He realized the only reason it hadn't been more was that most of his men were in the pass. They had been caught completely surprised.

Eldin watched the final Hussar flow past and stepped away from the mountain wall. Lifting his spear, he shouted, "With me, men! Spear Wall formation! Spear Wall!" Spears at the ready, they ran out of the pass. As he passed the now abandoned wagons, he couldn't help seeing the faces of his men who'd fallen, their empty eyes accusing him.

Eldin looked up to find the Hussars held a double ring around the clearing. But there were no raiders fighting them. In fact, the only raiders he could see were the handful that had fallen earlier. His squad stopped running, with no enemy in sight. He ordered them to combine squads to form a large shield wall. Then he went to find Paldabert.

"Lieutenant Paldabert! What's going on?" Eldin asked. "Where did the raiders go?"

"Good question," Paldabert returned. "As soon as we emerged, they rode south. We took a couple down before they could escape, but not one of them stayed around to fight. You needed us to secure the clearing, so I declined to pursue."

Eldin felt a cold shiver creep up his back. These Imzu weren't making any sense. How come he hadn't seen them when his men were going into the pass? Why did they even attack? Why not just go raid nearby villages like they did twenty years ago? And then why retreat from this attack, allowing his men to get safely out of the pass?

Paldabert was still looking at him. Eldin decided it didn't matter why. He just needed to do his job well and the rest would take care of itself. "Let's start with a shield wall in the center, with Hussar columns on each side," Eldin declared. "Then we march after these raiders. How's that for your Hussars?"

Paldabert just nodded and wheeled his mount back toward his men. "Hussars! Columns of four!"

Eldin hustled back over to the last men emerging from the pass. On the way, he barked at a soldier, "You call that a shield wall? Close that gap!"

There had been too many mistakes already. If ever Eldin needed to be precise, it was today.

Paldabert cantered over and pulled up next to Eldin. "My scouts have sighted the raiders. Estimated thirty men, to the southeast."

Eldin looked in that direction. "Are they holding or running?"

"They appear to be forming up on a nearby hill."

"Then I think we should take that hill. What do you think, Lieutenant?"

"Agreed." Paldabert pressed his mount into a run and sounded his own horn. The sound drew a cheer from the soldiers and in record time the entire Bolinian force was charging the hill. Exotic warriors wearing loose white robes waited for them, black steeds stamping the ground nervously. But at the last minute, the Imzu turned and raced down the backside of the hill. Frustrated, the Hussar cavalry picked up their pace, quickly leaving behind Eldin and the other spearmen. But just when Eldin considered calling a halt, he spotted a flash of black off to his left. Imzu horses raced away from them, between the hills, not far from his position. They were trying to flank his men and return to the pass.

"Sergeant Kamid," Eldin barked, "Third and Fourth Company are with you. Hold this position. We need our rear secure." He didn't wait for an answer. "First Company! Second Company! With me!"

The raiders had made a mistake coming onto his land. He had been patrolling these hills for fifteen years. He knew every wrinkle, including where the valley they were following would take them and a faster way to get to that point. If he could get there ahead of them, he might be able to trap them between a wall of spears to their front and charging Hussars from behind.

A man near Sergeant Kamid lowered his shield to the ground. Kamid walked over and kicked him in the back. "Keep your shield up, puke-face!"

Eldin had left him behind. The Imzu were out there, riding through his land, and he was guarding the top of an empty path. It should be him out there finishing off the raiders. The fact that they had to fight like this was Eldin's fault anyway. The idiot had gone on and on about wagons and stable cleaning.

Who knows? Maybe he'd get lucky and Eldin would be killed while chasing the Imzu. If they were going to actually be fighting Imzu, and not just running patrols, they'd need a real fighter in charge. And everyone knew Kamid was the best soldier in the fort.

Another man lowered his shield and Kamid kicked him, too. "Don't get lazy on me, ladies! I'm not dying because one of you is out of position when they charge us!"

Secretly, he understood. It was boring as all get out, waiting like this. And while their position on the hill that sloped up toward the fort was great for defense, it also provided no shade. And it was getting hot. He wanted the Imzu to get here already.

And then a pack of Imzu mongrels trotted on their horses around the path. That didn't make sense. They were riding toward him from the wrong direction. Seeing Kamid's line of soldiers, they halted.

"That's right!" Kamid shouted at them. He had about forty-five men to their thirty. "Thought you could get away from our Hussars! Well, we're ready for you!"

"Sir," a soldier quietly interrupted, "I don't think that's the same group that ran away this morning."

Kamid shot him a nasty look. "How would you know, moron? They all look the same." He turned back to the Imzu. "Come on! You want to try me now? You're not so brave when we're ready for you!"

Kamid's men shifted their feet and glanced back and forth between Kamid and the Imzu.

"See how scared they are, men?" Kamid spoke loudly enough that the Imzu could hear him address his men. "These dogs know what will happen if they try to fight real men! Run back to your caves, you cowards!"

A couple of the Imzu leaned close and talked with each other. One of them had a disgusting red beard. This one looked Kamid in the eye from across the field, "I know you! You were knocked on your backside and running from my men! I think it is you who are the coward! I think it is you who hides behind a wall of men and refuses to come and fight!"

"I am not afraid of you!" Kamid's face flushed hot. "Come here and say that to my face!"

The bearded Imzu laughed, a booming, arrogant laugh, and Kamid growled.

"I see why you hide behind your men, coward! You do not dare to leave your hill. You know I will knock you on your backside again! And this time I will kill you!"

"Forward march!" Kamid bellowed. His men just stared at him and so he started kicking everyone in range. "I said march, you mules!"

Reluctantly, his men began to move down the hill toward the waiting Imzu.

"Lower that spear!" Kamid snapped at a soldier to his left. "Let's put these dogs down! Double time!"

His men obediently started jogging, the tips of their spears bobbing up and down as they got closer and closer to the Imzu. Strangely, the Imzu weren't moving. The main advantage of cavalry over infantry came when charging at high speeds. Fine with him. If they were too stupid to fight properly it would only make killing them easier.

When they got within ten yards the cowards turned and rode away. Kamid grinned. Let them run. They were heading right into an enclosed ravine. He would corner them like the animals they were and slaughter them one by one.

He shouted in exultation and his men joined him.

He chased them around the curve, eager to see the look on their faces when they discovered the dead end. And then a massive rock flew past him, smashing into the line of soldiers a few feet to Kamid's right.

Kamid looked over to find nearly a dozen of his men dead or broken. Where had that come from?! Everyone knew the Imzu were ignorant savages.

His men shouted—a very different shout, this time—and he whipped his head back front, just in time to see another large rock hurtling right at him. His eyes widened. He couldn't do anything but stare and scream. Time slowed and his blood pounded in his ears. No way he died like this! This wasn't how it was supposed to be!

The second boulder hit the ground a spear-length in front of him, spraying dirt and grass in his face. It bounced just high enough to collide with Kamid's left hip. His hip bone cracked and his left leg snapped under the sudden pressure. Barely slowed by his body, the rock ripped into his side and exposed his organs to the air. Kamid fell on his back, eyes wide with shock. The pounding in his head grew quieter as his blood fled his body. The last thing he heard was the Imzu rider's laughter.

Eldin ran down the path as fast as he could, urging his men to keep up. This trail narrowed sharply just ahead. They needed to reach it before the Imzu if they wanted this ambush to work. Another ten minutes later they reached it. And only a couple of minutes after that someone shouted and Eldin glimpsed twenty dark-coated steeds coming around the bend to their right. But this was a smaller group than they'd been waiting for. The invaders must have split up once the Hussars started chasing them. That was fine with him. Taking them out one little group at a time was just fine with him.

And then he saw another group flash over a hill to his right, running perpendicular from where he and his men sat crouched behind boulders and bushes. Was that the rest of the group? Or another group? The two groups were heading in the same general direction. They might even be trying to set up the same trap he was working on—one enemy chasing you into an ambush force. Too bad for them he knew the land better than they did. The path this second group followed circled around to a dead end.

This was a golden opportunity to catch them in an enclosed space, where their horses wouldn't do them much good. But he still had some Imzu coming straight for him. He pounded his spear butt into the ground and thought. Which was more important? Maybe he didn't have to choose. "Corporal Bartek! Take Third Company and follow that group to our right and pin them up against the cliff at the end of the pass! Hold them there—do not let them come back this way. Keep your formations tight! Do not get sloppy!"

Third Company broke off and started marching to the spot he indicated.

"Stay hidden until the Imzu pass that boulder there," Eldin pointed to a spot about 10 yards down the trail. Then we step out as a group. Shield wall, each side facing the center, two ranks of spears behind each shield." He was quiet, but firm. The Imzu would be there any second. "We stop them here."

His men grinned wickedly.

Only few moments later, twenty riders came around the bend. Just as they reached the boulder, Eldin and his men jumped into the pass. Horses collided with shields and spears. A few Bolinians went down under the weight of a horse, but more than a few Imzu fell. Seeing their front ranks collapse, the rest of the Imzu pulled hard on their reins. Eldin shifted his grip on his shield and prepared for their attach. But they just turned around and left their fallen men behind. Eldin snarled. They were just going to run away again? Why wouldn't this group of raiders fight?

And then he realized, if these were the same Imzu the Hussars were chasing, why weren't the Hussars coming right behind them? And who was Third Company trying to trap? There were too many Imzu. Thirty Imzu had been in the first attack near the mouth of the pass. And there were about twenty Imzu in this group. And about ten in the other group. What if there weren't just thirty Imzu on this side of the pass? They had fled from the Hussars toward the south, but this group was heading northeast. Where had the first group run to? This close to the fort, there weren't that many places to hide—the fort!

What if there were a lot more than thirty?

Eldin sounded his horn as loud as he could. "To the fort! To the fort!" His men looked at him, confused. He started running and blew it again, hoping Third Company would hear and understand.

When they'd been ambushed while he was stuck in the pass, he had reacted in anger and chased after the first group of Imzu he'd seen, drawing him southeast—directly away from the fort. Eldin couldn't believe how stupid he'd been. It wasn't the Imzu who were splintering off into little groups, making it easy to pick them off one by one. Worse still, in all his efforts set up good positions, he had allowed himself to be lured away from the one position he most needed to protect.

He ran as fast as he possibly could. With deep dread, he realized he actually had no idea how many Imzu had crossed through the pass. They certainly had been given plenty of time to get through, while he was locked inside his fort rolling bedrolls.

It was a good thing he'd left Kamid behind to guard the path to the fort. At least he'd done something right.

CHAPTER SIX DEBRIEF

Eldin was confident that as long as he did his part well, it didn't matter what the Imzu were up to. He put his head down and focused on the work in front of his face. And he did those tasks with skill. Too bad they were the wrong tasks. If he would have looked up and considered what was going on around him, he might have been able to save the fort.

I do love strategy work. I probably spend more time than most planning for the future. But that didn't keep me from making this mistake, too. Once I spent months designing an epic development workshop and did only the minimum communication about the workshop to our target audience. It's really hard to help people if they don't show up. I learned the hard way my plan was fatally flawed.

I've come to believe that planning is the most important things leaders do. There are many skills great leaders must master. But being able to motivate people or assemble the right combination of people and resources, for example, assumes the target we're aiming at is the right one. Peter Drucker, the father of modern leadership and management consulting, said the most important thing leaders do is decide who does what. Warren Buffet, the world's most famous investor, said what makes someone great is saying "no" to ninety-nine good opportunities, investing only in the very best opportunity. I could go on and on with more quotes from the great men and women of history. No one leads well and misses this truth.

Make time to pull away from the many urgent tasks demanding your attention and focus on what's truly important. Not all tasks, projects, or strategies are equally important. The Pareto Principle, more often called the 80/20 Rule explains that about 80% of your results will come from

20% of your activities. So be careful not to fall into to the trap of evenly spreading yourself out, dedicating a little effort to many ideas. Do what the best do and focus on the critical few. Don't make Eldin's mistake and forget the fort.

DISCUSSION QUESTIONS

1. How often do you step away from the day to day tasks and think about what's most important?
2. What are the critical few things that get your organization the most results?
3. What most often distracts you from doing important planning?
4. How could you reduce the frequency and/or intensity of these distractions?

ACTION IDEA

Imagine your organization failed. Write out a summary of the most possible ways that could happen. What key resource was missing or unsupported? What partner didn't do what you expected? How did you get out of touch with your customers/clients on what key issues? For each possible problem you identify, rate how likely it is to happen. After getting this all on the table, create a plan to prevent each problem from blocking your success.

How To Fail as a Leader

BONUS QUESTIONS

5. In the chaos of the ambush, Eldin lost contact with his troops. How do you make sure your team stays in touch and up to date with each other?
6. Kamid's assumptions that the Imzu were inferior cost them all dearly. What assumptions are you making about your competition? About your own people?

My answers to many of these questions can be found on my blog. To join the discussion visit www.ScottWozniak.com

CHATPER SEVEN

Eldin and his men ran as fast as they could and no one worried about proper formation. While he ran he replayed his failures. While his men had been loading supply wagons, the Imzu must have crept through the pass and set up an ambush. They'd played him for a fool. They had dangled a squad of riders and he had followed right after them. Oh, but don't worry, he had run in the wrong direction with perfect technique!

Breathing hard, Eldin came in sight of the fort. It was worse than he had feared. He had prepared himself for Imzu horsemen massed at the front, maybe trying to climb ropes over the walls. Instead, he saw a large battering ram, supported by catapults on either side. The gates that had stood open for a decade were broken and bent inward..

What were Imzu nomads doing with siege weapons? Not in his worst nightmare had he thought they'd have siege engines. The Imzu had never used anything like this before.

But he'd been right about the Imzu massed outside the gates. Being wrong about that part would have been nice.

Twenty-two Imzu warriors turned from where they stood next to the siege machines and cried out. The raised swords and the entire group charged toward him. Eldin raised his shield and set his spear. And before they had covered ten yards, another thirty spearmen joined Eldin, with more pouring over the hill.

Eldin stared at the broken gates of his home one more moment and then a longsword slashed toward his neck. Years of training kicked in and his world narrowed to the enemy in front of him. Ducking down, keeping his feet planted beneath him, he brought his spear up a bit more. The sword missed him by less than an inch as the Imzu rode by. Eldin didn't miss.

Kicking the raider's body off his spearhead, he lunged forward to thrust at another Imzu engaged with the spearman to his right. His spear bit into the Imzu's arm and the raider was finished off quickly by another spearman next to Eldin. For the next few minutes, survival consumed everyone's attention. But as suddenly as it began, it was over.

Eldin had lost another thirteen men, but the entire enemy force had been killed. Pinned against the gates and overwhelmed, they didn't have a chance to use their superior speed. This kind of fighting was exactly what Bolinian spearmen trained for. It was about time something worked the way it should. His men looked around and then a ragged cheer went up. Eldin rested the butt of his spear on the ground, trying to catch his breath.

Eldin couldn't bring himself to cheer. They weren't done yet. Not by a long shot.

Black columns of smoke rose from inside the fort and he could see bodies inside the gates. Whose, he couldn't tell through the smoke. That meant there were more Imzu inside the fort. And he had injured men still in there. At least, he hoped there were men to rescue still in there.

"Running Diamond formation. Three groups, five yards apart." he barked. Signaling them to move forward, Eldin did something he never imagined he would do. He led an attack on his own fort.

They passed through the gates without being challenged and Eldin thrust his fist up, signaling a halt. Smoke filled the fort. Some spots were worse than others, but visibility was poor everywhere. Eldin signaled them to move forward again. They passed the first few buildings, both burning with doors smashed.

Three Bolinian men had been killed just inside the gates. Behind the first row of buildings he found three more. Another two lay around the next corner, making eight corpses. Still no sign of the invaders. Only one corpse wore white robes while seven had Bolinian brown. There weren't many men left defending the fort.

In the distance, he heard the distinctive neighing of a warhorse. He lifted his spear to the ready position, waiting for black horses to charge at them. He and his men waited, peering into the smoke, but nothing came toward them. After another long moment, Eldin gestured forward and they started walking, spears still at the ready.

Skirting around the building to the right, they reached the main stables. The entire group could hear a terrible commotion, including the horrible squeal of a distressed horse. Eldin pulled the door open and stuck his head in. Who was fighting in the stables? Had Addoc and the stablemaster returned?

"Birn? Birn? It's Eldin!" He turned back to the men. "Fourth and Fifth Squad, continue to follow the outer wall around the fort. Make for the infirmary. Second and Third Squad, take a more central path, but head to the same place. First Squad, hold this position while I scout this sound."

He stepped inside. "Birn. If you're in here, come out!" He could see fire at the end of the long hallway—and no one else. The flames hadn't reached the hay bales yet, but they were dangerously close. The stable wouldn't last much longer after that happened. He sprinted to the stablemaster's tack room in the middle of the stables. He didn't know if he was more relieved or disappointed to find it empty. Smoke was filling the hallway but he went a bit further anyway. The thumps and squeals of a warhorse was very close, now. Sure enough, he found a horse frantically kicking the door to its stall. Coughing a bit from the smoke, Eldin smashed the door open and jumped out the way. Desperate to get away from the flames, the huge animal burst out of the stall and ran away from the flames, back the way Eldin had come.

Eldin followed after the horse without even looking in any of the other stalls. He knew for sure that Birn wasn't here, now. There was no way Birn would have left that horse alone if he was nearby. And that was good, because wherever Birn was had to be safer than this.

The large, light gray horse reached the end of the row at a run and kicked the partially open door, smashing it all the way open. Shouts erupted on the other side and Eldin sprinted forward. The thick stable doors had slammed into one of his men and hit the side of an Imzu horse and rider. It knocked the Bolinian down and threw off the Imzu's balance. The invader, thwarted for the moment, spurred his horse and charged into the smoke. The escaping steed just kept running, disappearing into the smoke-filled walkway between the buildings. The five soldiers Eldin had left to guard the door were trying to form a tiny wall of spears, swinging their weapons back and forth at every shadow in the smoke. There weren't enough of his men to protect from every direction.

Just as Eldin reached his men, eight Imzu riders emerged from the smoke as a group, moving steadily for them. Eldin considered retreating into the stables, but it had caught fire. It was going to get ugly in there real fast. Eldin considered his options and came up with nothing. It was going to get ugly whatever he did. He adjusted his grip on his spear and steeled himself to take a few Imzu down with him.

Then a Hussar burst out of the smoke from behind the Imzu at a full gallop, wielding a standard Hussar blade and a long, thin sword, one in each hand. His huge gray horse plowed into the flank of a smaller desert horse, knocking him into another rider. The Hussar kept moving forward, passing them as they tried to recover their balance. His swords slashed, one to the right and the other to the left. With each stroke, an Imzu fell. Still charging forward, he crashed into another white robed raider at the front of the pack. The tall, gray warhorse kicked out. The smaller brown horse staggered and Breakaway's hooves crushed the side of the rider, dropping him immediately. The Bolinian wheeled around, and in the moment before launching back into motion, Eldin recognized him.

Addoc crouched in his stirrups and pointed his blades at his new targets. His first pass through the Imzu had distracted one and killed three Imzu. The others began to spread out, the infantry all but forgotten in the face of this new threat. Addoc didn't wait for them to reform, though, thundering forward. As he neared, the Imzu swung his blade at Breakaway's face, trying to distract the warhorse. Instead, Breakaway just ducked his head without slowing. The Imzu didn't pull his arm back fast enough and Addoc's sword took his hand off. Without looking back at the screaming man, Addoc directed Breakaway to the left to race at three more raiders—who jerked their mounts' heads around and fled into the smoke.

Addoc pulled up and turned to Eldin. "How many men are with you?"

"Three squads. I sent the other two squads to the infirmary."

Addoc clenched his teeth. "Too late. I just came from there. It was the first place I looked."

"Anyone?"

Addoc shook his head. "All dead." Addoc suddenly coughed. The smoke was getting thicker, especially up where Addoc was perched. He recovered the ability to speak and declared in a hoarse voice, "It won't be long until the rest of the fort burns. We need to gather the men we have left and regroup outside. There's nothing left to defend here."

Twenty minutes later, Addoc swung his sword down with all his might. Then did it again. They hadn't seen anyone else, friend or foe, on the way out of the fort. Several times more, he slammed a longsword he'd confiscated from one of the fallen invaders down onto a joint at the base of a wooden catapult. They couldn't take the big, slow siege engines with them. But they couldn't leave them behind for the enemy either. He chopped away at the point where two wooden beams were nailed together. It was the only thing holding the last catapult up. All the other war machines had been broken by Eldin and the other soldiers. This was the last one standing.

The sound of metal smacking hardwood made him wince. He paused and lifted the sword to check the edge. Swords, even those as finely made as this one, weren't made for chopping wood. Being used this way had blunted the edge so badly that Addoc didn't think it was cutting the wood anymore. Addoc glared at the ruined sword. It suddenly seemed like a symbol for all that had happened to him. All his hopes, all his naive dreams about his leadership…ruined. He clenched his teeth hard and bashed the sword against the wood. It didn't do any good.

No. He refused to give up. He would not fail! He jammed the tip of the sword into the joint and pulled back. Just because it couldn't cut didn't mean it was useless. It didn't budge. He gripped it tighter with both hands and heaved with his whole body. For a second, he felt the wood give. And then, with an ugly snap the blade broke. Addoc staggered back and stared at what was left of the sword. A few inches past the hilt, the metal ended in a ragged, ugly edge. For a moment, it felt like his will to fight had broken along with the sword.

Edlin walked past Addoc and wedged his spear into the same spot. Since all the other catapults were broken, he might as well help. He pulled back and the wood groaned, but it still wasn't enough. Addoc sighed and dropped the broken sword on the ground. He trudged over to Eldin and grabbed the end of the spear. "On three?" Addoc asked. Eldin nodded. They counted to three then strained together. The wood wailed one more time and the last joint fell apart.

Addoc and Eldin jumped back as the catapult collapsed under its own weight. There were more Imzu out in the hills, somewhere. With the large machines destroyed, the Bolinians were free to move on.

"Let's go," Addoc said to Eldin.

Eldin barked, "Move out!"

Addoc suddenly decided to pick the broken hilt back up. Holding in in one hand, he used the other to swing onto Breakaway's back. From his high position he surveyed his troops as they began marching. Spearmen, mostly, with a few archers. He rode the only horse in the group. He took a deep breath and trotted Breakaway up to the front of the line, slowing to match Eldin's pace.

Eldin looked up at him. "Where's the stablemaster, sir?"

Addoc kept his eyes forward. "I've seen these engines before."

"Sure. These are the same engines that were here when we entered the fort," Eldin assured him. "Where's Birn, sir? Did you leave him at Robik?"

"I didn't go to the village, Sergeant." Addoc turned away from the catapult to face Eldin. "And I don't mean these exact engines. I mean I've seen engines just like this—the same design."

"So where *is* the stablemaster?" Eldin persisted.

Addoc snapped, "He's buried in a ravine about a mile to the south."

"He's dead?" Eldin blurted.

"I wouldn't have buried him alive," Addoc shot back.

"I knew taking him to the Imzu would kill him!" Eldin accused.

"It wasn't the Imzu! It was our own men!" Addoc shouted.

Eldin stopped walking, then had to jog to catch back up. "But he was fine when you took him away!"

"Someone shot him before I'd gone twenty yards from the gate," Addoc corrected bitterly.

"Was it Kamid?" Eldin demanded. "If it was Kamid—"

"I don't know who it was," Addoc interrupted. He clenched his jaw and after a moment he explained. "We were riding away and an arrow struck him in the back. When he fell off Breakaway it tore open the wound. He bled out pretty quickly after that."

"I—I'm sorry to hear that, sir."

"Yeah. He was a good kid." They walked in awkward silence for a moment.

"How did the Imzu get inside the fort?" Addoc suddenly said. "And where are the rest of the men?"

Eldin swallowed and looked down. "I left Kamid to guard this path with Third and Fourth Companies. I have no idea where he is. Last I saw, Lieutenant Paldabert and the Hussars were pursuing a group of Imzu riders, heading southeast. I—I also have no idea where they are."

"How did this happen? Where did *you* go?" Addoc pressed.

"The Imzu must have come through during the pass yesterday. So when we marched out—we were going to set up camp on their side—well, they waited until we got deep into the pass and attacked the rear of our line."

"You left the fort unguarded?" Addoc's voice dripped with scorn.

"I didn't," Eldin declared. "Sergeant Kamid was supposed to guard the path to the fort while we chased down the invaders. When I came back, I found, well, you saw it."

"But why would you march out if the Imzu had come through the pass? Didn't any of yesterday's patrols see them come through the pass?" Addoc couldn't understand what Eldin had been thinking.

Eldin swallowed. "I was so focused on getting ready for our attack that I didn't consider what the Imzu were planning. I told everyone to prepare for the march."

"I told you we shouldn't invade!" Addoc shouted. "What kind of leader leaves his fort empty and chases after light cavalry?"

"At least I was here!" Eldin shot back. "You left us, *sir*."

"I thought you could handle things while I was gone," Addoc defended. "I guess I was wrong."

Eldin clamped his mouth shut, keeping in whatever he'd been about to say. After a tense moment, Eldin asked, "What did the Imzu say?"

"Excuse me?" Addoc was confused, and still angry.

"You went to speak with them, to try to stop a war. Did you find them? What did they say?"

Addoc heaved a sigh and rubbed his eyes for a moment. In the face of his own failures, it was hard to sustain his indignation. Finally, he spoke. "I was wrong about that, too."

"Sir?"

"I did speak with their war leader." Addoc explained. "Big fellow, red beard. And it didn't do any good. He had already decided to attack. They even tried to kill me, even though I was under a flag of truce. I've been wrong about a lot, Sergeant." He took a deep breath. "I'm sorry…for a lot of things."

Eldin looked at Addoc for a long moment. Then he shook his head and looked down. "Yeah, I'm sorry, too, sir."

They traveled in silence for a while.

Eldin grunted out a bitter laugh. "If you combine the two of us, sir, I think we've made just about every leadership mistake possible."

Addoc laughed, then turned toward Eldin. "You know, Sergeant, you might be on to something."

"Sir?"

"I thought being a leader was all about having a great vision and being creative. And you focused on making sure everything was done with excellence. I thought the details didn't matter. And you thought that details were all that mattered. We were both wrong. But we were also both right. If we could work together, combine our strengths…" he paused, turning to Eldin. "But we'll have to work together this time. Really work together."

Eldin looked him in the eye. "I'm willing to give it a try, if you are, sir."

Addoc smiled. "Deal."

"Remember how I told you I'd seen those catapult designs before?" Addoc asked after another moment.

Eldin nodded.

"I saw them used against us by Shelish troops," Addoc explained. "How would nomads like the Imzu get their hands on catapults designed by Shel? Doesn't that strike you as odd?"

"Siege engines are pretty odd for a nomad culture to use," Eldin admitted.

"And if all this was a reaction to us marching onto their land," Addoc went on, "how would they have time to build siege engines?" Addoc held out what was left of this broken longsword. "Do you recognize this sword?"

"Never seen it before."

"I have. Or at least I've seen swords just like it back east. This is a Shelish longsword."

"So, the Imzu are using Shelish-designed catapults and Shelish swords," Eldin summarized.

"And breaking a peace twenty-years old at the same time the Shel are invading in the east," Addoc added. "Quite a coincidence, don't you think?"

"So the plan was to destroy our fort all along?"

"I don't know. Shel wouldn't really care about Fort Highrock—this fort is as removed from the war as you can get. But there is something less than a day's ride from here that they are depending on in the east."

"The supply depot in Robik!" Eldin exclaimed. "Sir! We need to pull everyone back there to defend the village."

"We may be all that's left. If Paldabert and Kamid haven't returned, we have to assume something is keeping them from returning."

"It would take a lot of Imzu to wipe out both of them and their troops." Eldin couldn't help looking around, even though he knew he wouldn't be able to see anything beyond the valley they were walking through.

"Even if our men are still out there," Addoc added, "we can't wait for them. We have to fortify the village immediately. It's up to us to defend the army supply depot," Addoc declared.

"But how do we stop what could be an army of invaders with only fifty or so men?"

"I do have an idea," Addoc offered. "It's a little crazy—maybe even really crazy—but with your help, it might just work."

CHAPTER SEVEN DEBRIEF

Addoc believed if he inspired people with a grand vision, he didn't need to get bogged down in the details. So, he considered strategy and left the day-to-day management to others, sure that as long as they had the best strategy the little things would work themselves out. Eldin thought whoever had the most discipline and skill should be the leader. So, he made all the decisions and solved all the problems, trusting that if he worked with excellence he would win in the end. Who was right about leadership?

Neither. And both.

Addoc learned the hard way that that leadership depends on details done well. Every great idea eventually degenerates into hard work. Eldin discovered, also the hard way, that being the best worker doesn't make you the best leader. There is no benefit in doing the wrong things well. They eventually learned that good leaders don't choose vision or precision.

When faced with a choice between two competing priorities, it's tempting to choose one perspective over another. But some tensions aren't supposed to be solved. Some tensions must be managed. Allowing one side to win will create more problems than it solves. We have to live with the tension, doing the hard work of keeping them both important.

Leadership is not about great vision or great precision. It's both.

You probably have a natural tendency toward one mode or another. Most of us do. If so, you'll need to compensate for your bias. That might mean hiring someone who excels in what you lack, or scheduling regular time to think in the mode you usually don't use. You might need to use checklists to make sure no details are missed. You might need to engage a coach to stretch your strategic thinking. There are a lot of options. Find some way to incorporate the other perspective into your leadership.

Remember, leading means rising above your personal preferences and doing what serves those you lead. You don't have to become a different person. But you're not stuck with your current abilities either. I've erred on both sides of the issue. I have been the creative but sloppy leader, spending hours on the graphic design of a presentation handout, then showing up late for the presentation. I've also worked for 70 hours, week after week, while those I led stood around asking for more work. I'm hoping that my failures will be your lessons, that you can dodge a few of the traps I stepped into. If I can grow and change, so can you.

DISCUSSION QUESTIONS

1. Are you more likely to make Eldin's mistakes (put your head down and do it all yourself) or Addoc's mistakes (dream up new ideas and ignore the details)?
2. What is your method for making sure others work with excellence? (*If you're in a discussion group and this isn't your strength, you might want to take notes when others share their ideas.*)
3. Where do you go to get new ideas? (*Again, if this isn't your strength, take good notes when others in your discussion group answer.*)

ACTION IDEA

Go to ScottWozniak.com/howtofailasaleader and take the assessment on your leadership style. Then send the link for the assessment to 3-5 people who work with you and ask them to rate you as well. Compare your answers to theirs. Identify one way you can more often use one of your strengths. Identify one thing you can do to improve a weakness.

BONUS QUESTIONS

4. Eldin wanted a high level of certainty before making a decision, while Addoc was willing to act on a hunch. From 0%-100%, how much certainty do you need to have before you are comfortable deciding? (E.g. you have to be 70% sure you're right before you will act—or 95% sure.)
5. What are the advantages of waiting for more information?
6. What are the advantages of acting quickly?

My answers to many of these questions can be found on my blog. To join the discussion visit www.ScottWozniak.com

CHAPTER EIGHT

When they reached Robik, Eldin arranged rooms for the night for their exhausted men. A dozen took rooms at the small inn, including Addoc, but the rest stayed with the friends and family of Eldin. Within an hour, every one of their men was asleep.

Except for Eldin and Addoc.

They went to the kitchen in Eldin's parents' house to plan. Addoc laid out his grand idea and Eldin immediately noticed flaws. He almost didn't speak up, but Addoc pressed him to point out what was missing. He saw several problems, not the least was that Addoc's plan included tearing up parts of the village. Eldin pointed out a few flaws and braced himself for Addoc's condescending reply. Addoc didn't exactly smile, but neither did he dismiss Eldin's concerns outright. In fact, he wrote them down and asked if Eldin had any other concerns. When Eldin had finished naming all the problems he could see, which ended up being a long list, they worked through the list item by item, finding solutions. Addoc's solutions often began with wild ideas, citing books he'd read, war stories heard from his father's friends, and sometimes it seemed like he pulled ideas out of thin air. Again and again, Eldin said it wouldn't work. More than once, Eldin had to press Addoc to be more specific. It got heated more than once. But they didn't quit. They couldn't afford to. Too much depended on finding a real solution. And Eldin had to admit, some of Addoc's ridiculous ideas were pretty clever. Besides, they didn't have much chance using traditional military methods.

Morning came and they hadn't slept. But they did have a plan. Eldin leaned back and rubbed his eyes. "You know this is crazy, right? The Imzu might not even be heading toward the supply depot. They might already be on their way back home. If we do all this and they don't come—"

"We can't take that chance," Addoc said yet again. "If they do come and we aren't ready..."

"I know, I know. I didn't say I wasn't going to help. I just said this is crazy."

Addoc grinned and said, "Great leaders do things that have never been done before, right?"

A tired smile crept over Eldin's face. "Let's see if this works and then decide whether it was good leadership or not."

At sunrise, they woke the forty-five surviving soldiers of Fort Highrock and gathered in the village square. Eldin and Addoc stood out front, side by side. Addoc spoke loudly. "Yesterday, we escaped with our lives. You probably noticed that Imzu aren't raiding and retreating like they have in the past. In fact, we believe the Imzu are on their way here to attack the supply depots we use to support the war out east. Our enemy is doing things they've never done before. That means we've got to do something different, too. "

"Who says they're coming here?" one of the men mumbled under his breath.

"I do," thundered Eldin. "Listen to him, you bunch of mules. Some of you saw him fight yesterday. And you know who his father is." Heads nodded grudgingly. "Our Captain has seen more battle out east than all of us put together. And I've been up all night with him planning this. What he's about to share is not just his plan. It's my plan, too."

Addoc gratefully nodded at Eldin. "Up until now, we thought the Imzu only wanted to loot and leave, like they always have. But I need you to think bigger. What if they're after a richer prize than these villages? What if their target wasn't our fort? What if the Imzu could cross the bridge at the end of this street?" Addoc pointed to his right. "And what could they do after setting fire to our supply depot? Imagine more than a hundred Imzu raiding the farms of western Bolin—while our entire army is focused back east on Shel. But we have a chance to stop them, right here, right now, before they can do any of that. This isn't going to be easy. And I could be wrong about all of this. But I need you to trust me. Because if I'm right, what you do today could save our nation."

"And I need you to do your work exactly right!" Eldin interjected. "Small mistakes could get all of us killed, so pay attention!"

Noon came and went and still no one had approached the village of Robik. Eldin's credibility in his home village had allowed them to do a lot of strange things during the morning. But as the sun started to slide toward the western mountains, the villagers began to wonder if they'd let these soldiers ruin their town for no reason. And the villagers weren't the only ones having doubts.

Addoc, Eldin, and about twenty-five men waited in a field a hundred yards west of the village. One of the men mumbled, "They aren't coming."

"You don't move a hundred and fifty men quickly," Eldin returned. He didn't know if the Imzu had that many. That was larger than any other raiding party the Imzu had sent through the pass before. But Eldin insisted they prepare for the worst scenario.

They all returned to staring at the crest of a hill further out, where one of their scouts lay hidden in tall grass.

Suddenly, the scout scrambled backwards on his stomach, then started running toward them in a crouch. "They're here!"

As the man approached, Eldin asked, "How many?" He would be so glad to be wrong this time. Please, let it less than a hundred.

"Maybe two or three hundred, sir! I couldn't count them all!"

Addoc and Eldin looked at each other.

"Do you think we have time to make any changes?" Addoc asked. "Maybe add some pits?"

"We should work the plan, sir. Any last minute changes could interfere with what we've already done."

Addoc grimaced, but nodded. "Agreed."

Eldin turned to the scout, "Well done, soldier. Go join the others." The scout dashed back to the village.

Addoc mounted Breakaway, and then rode away from the village, to the crest of the hill. When he reached the top, he spurred Breakaway, causing him to rear up on his hind legs and Addoc screamed. His mouth went dry when he saw the mass of mounted warriors only a few hundred yards away. Cries went out when they saw him and for a split second he wanted to turn and run. But instead he shouted, "Imzu! I am what you fear in the night! I am the Hussar that makes you tremble and cry! If you do not leave now, I will kill every last one of you!"

The answering roar from the Imzu was louder than Addoc was ready for. For better and for worse, the challenge was issued. The fear on Addoc's face wasn't feigned. He spun Breakaway around and they rode back down the hill, toward Robik.

The men who had been waiting with him, including Eldin, were already running toward the village. They had been chosen in part for their speed as runners and they pushed themselves as fast as they could. As Addoc approached them, he looked over his shoulder and saw a flood of black and brown Imzu steeds pouring over the top of the hill. They kept coming and coming and coming. He didn't know if their plan would still work with that many Imzu.

Addoc spurred Breakaway and quickly rode past Eldin and the other men. "See you at the river!" Addoc shouted. The rumble of the hundreds and hundreds of hooves behind them could be felt. They passed a side street blocked by hay-filled wagons. Two soldiers stationed there shoved burning torches into the hay. Then Eldin ran past the next side street and the next pair of spearmen lit another blockade of wagons on fire.

What the Imzu warriors saw was an arrogant Hussar and twenty-five soldiers running away. For years, they had heard stories of the terrible might of the Hussars. But in the last few days, they had beaten these legends. And now, the Bolinian dogs ran before them into the strange village of wooden tents. The front riders laughed out loud. No trenches, no walls, nothing stood between them and the running Bolinians. They lifted their swords and whooped. The men raced to be the first to draw blood. Twenty yards out from the first building, their canter became a gallop. Soon a stampede of Imzu warriors poured onto the main street of Robik, only yards behind the fleeing soldiers.

Zishwae rode in very front, as befit a great war leader. The wind tossed his red beard around and he grinned fiercely, savoring his victory already. He was almost upon the slowest of the Bolinians. The fires they were passing confused him, but didn't concern him. He was planning to burn this village anyway. Caught up in the glory and fury of chasing prey, he didn't think too much about it. Crushing these soft Bolinians was going to be even easier than the ambassador from Shel had said!

He lifted his new longsword, still marveling at its light weight. Then the stone covered path he was following curved to the right and his arm froze in the air. He had heard of rivers before, but even in his imagination they hadn't been this big. He stared for a long moment at the rippling, rushing water. It was glorious—and terrifying. He'd never seen anything like it. He was still riding at full gallop when he noticed his path led straight into the water. Broken beams at the edge of the road marked where the wooden bridge of Robik had stood for almost two centuries. His prey—or, more accurately, the bait—ran straight to the water's edge and like complete madmen leaped into the wild rushing water. Instantly the water swept them away as their arms were pumped forward and back in some futile attempt to save themselves. But their faces were down as the river took them away. Zishwae wrote them off as already dead.

However insane the Bolinians were, the Imzu warrior had no plans of riding into the horrifying river. He pulled on the reins, but when his horse slowed, he was slammed into from behind. The tight mass of galloping warriors coming down the path behind him couldn't see what lay around the bend in the road. The nearby fires and growing smoke were making the horses harder to control as well. His horse lurched forward, reacting to being pressed from behind, and Zishwae found himself on the edge of a small cliff, teetering over more water than he'd ever seen in his life. Another wave of riders swept around the curve in the road, putting more pressure on the pile of horses clustered at the edge. And then Zishwae and his horse fell. He desperately tried to get his feet out of the stirrups. But he hit the water harder than he'd imagined was possible, one foot still tangled in the stirrups.

In thirty seconds, forty or fifty Imzu riders plummeted into the river. Men and animals both panicked, thrashing around wildly. A few Imzu had the sense to hang on to their horses. But then archers stepped out from the other side of the river and began to fire at them. A handful were soldiers from the fort, but many were villagers using their hunting bows. Most of the best aimed shots were coming from the villagers.

That still left more than two hundred Imzu in the streets for the rest of the Bolinian soldiers. Far more than they had anticipated. Some raiders were trampled as their warhorses collided at the end of the street. Then, as the stampede slowed and halted, the burning wagons that had waited in the side streets rolled out into the mass of men and beasts. Imzu horses reared away from the fire and both men and horses struggled to breathe in the smoke. Into the maelstrom, the remaining spearmen of Bolin charged from the houses and shops they'd been waiting in all day.

The smoke grew too thick to see more than ten or twelve feet away. Addoc used that to his advantage. Packed together between the buildings on either side of the road, the Imzu were unable to use the hit and run tactics they knew from desert warfare. On the other hand, close quarters combat was something the Bolinians had practiced for decades. It was ugly, bloody work. But in thirty minutes, though thirty-one Bolinians fell, they took nearly two hundred Imzu with them to the grave. Twenty-three riders at the rear of the Imzu charge managed to escape the massacre, scattering into the hills.

Soon, only Bolinians were left standing in the street, breathing hard and looking around in wonder. A soot-covered Eldin walked over to a blood-splattered Addoc.

"Burn the town to save it, huh?" Eldin remarked.

They both looked at the mess around them. The fire was spreading to some buildings and people had already begun to shift from fighting the Imzu to fighting the fires.

"I have to admit, I wasn't sure it would work." Eldin admitted. "If they hadn't taken the bait…"

"I guess their leader just isn't as good with details as I am," Addoc said. He even managed to keep a straight face.

Eldin rolled his eyes, but couldn't hold back his smirk as he replied. "It was my brilliant strategy that won the day, of course."

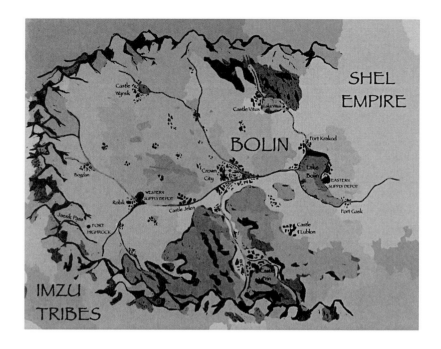

EPILOGUE

General Jolo, Supreme General of the Empire of Shel, leaned back in his chair and rubbed his eyes. In front of him lay a table full of maps, and the latest markings he had just added weren't good. The stubborn Bolinians were making him pay dearly for every inch of territory he'd won. Thanks to those cursed mountains there was only one real entry point into the nation. The Bolinians weren't dumb, unfortunately, and they'd filled that opening with forts and troops. And a frontal assault on fortified positions was also the most costly way to fight a war. Year after year, the Emperor delayed annexing the wealthy little nation. But General Jolo had finally convinced the Emperor that he could win. In fact, he had promised a quick win. And he shivered to think what could happen if he didn't deliver on that promise.

A gust of cold wind blasted into the tent, upsetting his maps. He looked up to find a messenger standing at the entrance, holding the door flap open.

"Get in here and close the flap," Jolo snarled.

The soldier approached. "Message for you, sir. Marked urgent."

The general broke the seal and read the note. Then he threw it on the table. The messenger waited, his gaze wisely on the floor.

"Tell Colonel Abru to gather all the officers for a war council—immediately!"

"Yes, sir." The messenger hurried out without looking up.

After all the trouble and expense he'd gone through to find a tribe of Imzu willing to attack—and then outfitting them—the stupid savages had failed to do any real damage in the west. One tiny, meaningless fort! They were supposed to destroy the western supply depot! Run wild in western end of the country! The general started pacing, working on how he would explain this to the Emperor of Shel. Someone was going to pay for this failure. He needed a new plan, and fast, or that someone would be him.

CHAPTER EIGHT DEBRIEF

It cuts deep when the finger of blame is pointed at me, again. My instincts demand I cover my ears, close my eyes and run as fast as possible; they scream at me to get through the moment and back to normal as fast as possible. I've done that many times. Eventually the sting fades and I can pretend it never happened. But over the years I discovered that buried in the pain is a chance to uncover a deep truth and make myself a better man, if I have the strength of character to embrace it.

I've come to believe one of the best measures of my character is how I respond when faced with my failure. Do I justify, excuse, and explain why it isn't really my fault? Do I lash out at those who are attacking me? Do I run away and hide until the trouble goes away? Or do I take responsibility for my choices? Do I look for the nugget of truth in the criticism, even when poorly given? Am I even open to admitting that I could be at fault?

I've been given a lot of chances to take this heart test. I'm not what most people would call a natural rule follower. That's led to being corrected many, many times, sometimes out of love for me, sometimes not. Too often I chose to attack, justify, or hide. I ran from the pain and wasted the chance to grow. But I remember vividly the first time I seriously considered the fault was mine. Oddly, I don't remember what the argument was about. But I do remember storming off to another room to pace, fuming. After a minute, I stopped and asked myself, "Could I actually be the one wrong here?" Time seemed to slow and I teetered on the edge of a choice. For some reason (I give the credit to God nudging me), I chose, for the first time, to let go of the assumption that I was right. I chose to open myself up to the shame of being wrong. And I grew.

I wish I could say I made a wise choice every time after that. But it did happen again. And each brave choice made it a little easier. I'm still making mistakes. It still hurts to discover what I've done wrong. But I'm not wasting the pain anymore.

Being a leader does not require being right all the time. Of course, if you're wrong all the time, you do have a real problem. But, assuming you're basically competent, acknowledging fault to your followers is actually a great opportunity to grow your influence. We fear our vulnerability will drive others away from us, but the opposite is true. Think about how we respond when someone else is humble and honest. I'm drawn to them, not repulsed. How the leader responds to failure has a big impact on how everyone else responds to failure. You can create an environment where failure isn't a shame to run from, but a chance to grow. You not only gain wisdom yourself, but you make it easier for those you lead to learn from failure.

Whoever loves discipline loves knowledge, but whoever hates correction is stupid. Proverbs 12:1

DISCUSSION QUESTIONS

1. Who could benefit from you teaching them some of the lessons you learned from this story? (One of the best ways to lock in what you've learned is to teach it.)
2. What is the first step you're going to take to improve your balance between vision and execution?
3. When will you take that first step?

ACTION IDEAS

- Share what you've learned with those you lead. If you need to acknowledge a mistake or just a change in thinking, do that. Certainly, tell them of any changes or new steps you plan to take.
- Invite someone to be a support partner as you change. Either find a peer who is working on similar leadership skills or hire a leadership coach to help you move from ideas to action. (If you don't know of any good coaches, contact me for some recommendations.)
- Invite a few others to join you in a discussion group, where you each read a chapter and meet to discuss the questions at the end, one chapter a week for eight weeks.

My answers to many of these questions can be found on my blog. To join the discussion visit
www.ScottWozniak.com

And please contact me anytime:
Scott@ScottWozniak.com
Twitter: ScottEWozniak
Facebook: facebook.com/ScottWozniakLeadership